CREATIVE ADVENTURES

EDITED BY BYRON TOBOLIK

First published in Great Britain in 2023 by:

Young Writers
Remus House
Coltsfoot Drive
Peterborough
PE2 9BF
Telephone: 01733 890066
Website: www.youngwriters.co.uk

Printed and bound in the UK by BookPrintingUK
Website: www.bookprintinguk.com
YB0538Z

Foreword

Welcome, Reader!

For our latest competition A Twist in the Tale, we challenged primary school students to write a story in just 100 words that will surprise the reader. They could add a twist to an existing tale, show us a new perspective or simply write an original story.

The authors in this anthology have given us some creative new perspectives on tales we thought we knew, and written stories that are sure to surprise! The result is a thrilling and absorbing collection of stories written in a variety of styles, and it's a testament to the creativity of these young authors. Be prepared for shock endings, unusual characters and amazing creativity!

Here at Young Writers it's our aim to inspire the next generation and instill in them a love of creative writing, and what better way than to see their work in print? The imagination and skill within these pages are proof that we might just be achieving that aim! Congratulations to each of these fantastic authors.

Contents

Ailsa McNeill (10)	63
Lexie Glen (10)	64
Eve McLetchie (10)	65
Colton Clark (10)	66
Jamie Adams (10)	67
Erin McLeod (11)	68
Reegan Muir (10)	69
Kacie Pratt (11)	70
Chloe Gardiner (10)	71
Libby Wilson (9)	72
Brooke Mason (9)	73
Jessica Davies (11)	74
Hunter Naismith (10)	75
Eve Madden (11)	76
Ross Thomson (10)	77
Jayden-James Mullen (11)	78
Jessie Obinna (10)	79
Emma McCutcheon (9)	80
Grace Brown (11)	81
Emma Paterson (10)	82
Hugo Smith (10)	83
Glen Cameron (11)	84
Brodie Murdoch (10)	85
Ella Nisbet (10)	86
Olivia Ferguson (10)	87
Thomas Mooney (11)	88
Macey Docherty (11)	89
Bailey Leishman (9)	90
Ellie Laird (11)	91
Dominic Roddie (10)	92
Eilidh Nicol (11)	93
Riley Brady (10)	94
Kaitlyn Daly (10)	95
Lucas Parker (11)	96
Alea Fowler (11)	97
Charlotte Binnie (11)	98
Matthew Farmer (11)	99
Rhoan Hendrie (11)	100
Jack Chapman (11)	101
Paige Babes (11)	102
Anna Cruickshanks (11)	103
Leo Forsyth (10)	104
Kayla Kinsella (9)	105
Harry Cunningham (10)	106
Mya Hunter (11)	107
Alan Steele (11)	108

Daniela Hunter (11)	109
Millie Forrest (11)	110
Megan Dargie (11)	111
Charlie Gray (10)	112
Jay Young (11)	113
Ava Brewer (10)	114
Lewis MacDonald (11)	115
Gregor McNeill (11)	116
Neve Clark (11)	117
Lacey Laird (11)	118

Dorridge Primary School, Dorridge

Oliver Mackay (9)	119
Indie Kirkbride (9)	120
Darcy Churchill (10) & Aarya Mistry	121
Katy Quest (9)	122
Izzy Mattine (7)	123
Elinor Smith (8)	124
Avaani Sandhar (9)	125
Ben Frowd (9)	126
Rosa Baillie (9)	127
Ben Quest (7)	128
Isaac Herd (9)	129
George Ward (9)	130
Elanor Liddiard (8)	131
Elizabeth Blight (9)	132
Charlie Ward (7)	133
Persia Athena Vassell (7)	134
Amber Nyland (9)	135
Emma Herd (7)	136
Orla Jackson (8)	137
Matty Pensom (7)	138
Samuel Hill (5)	139
Alexandria Hogan (9)	140
Dylan Campbell (8)	141
Mason Bains (8)	142

Edith Moorhouse Primary School, Carterton

Eliza-Mai Collings (11)	143
Joseph Cutler (10)	144
Tiffany Hutton (9)	145

Charlie Crutch (10)	146
Louie Paul (10)	147
Rosie Goodman (10)	148
Charlie Sprigg (10)	149
Finley Agar (9)	150
Jacob Austin (10)	151
Lily Price (10)	152

Homerswood Primary School, Kirklands

Holly Fairless Bush (10)	153
Annie Bailey (10)	154
Neve Kent (10)	155
Ruby-Mae Reed (11)	156
Joshua Bouma (10)	157
Luke Johnson (10)	158
Mia Dring (11)	159
Charlie Brewis (11)	160
Bethany Sperring (11)	161
Henry Robins (10)	162

Mauricewood Primary School, Greenlaw Mains

Rose Hand (9)	163
Marisa Harris-Mckenzie (9)	164
Lena Crooks (9)	165
Holly Lumber (9)	166
Kamya-do Caine (9)	167
Nicole Lister (9)	168
Lillian Mason (9)	169
Kai Steel (8)	170
Oliver Lavery (9)	171
Harrison Trang	172
Aimee Davidson (9)	173
Eli Lumsden	174
Connor Ewen (9)	175
Sophia Aird (8)	176
Mikolaj Szczesniak (9)	177
Mason Stafford (9)	178
Alex McCreadie (9)	179
Joseph Kirk (9)	180
Grace Gibb (8)	181
Sophia Pang (9)	182
Ruaridh Scott (9)	183

Jack Thorne (9)	184
Emeli White (9)	185
Emily Stewart (9)	186
Eve Hogarth (9)	187
Katie Fraser	188
Aiden Salt-Mayhew (9)	189
Walter Gray (9)	190
Emmy Allison (9)	191
Lily Chamberlain (9)	192
Charlie Newby (9)	193
Ayla Hill	194
Tamsin Dobie	195
Ella Vakaloloma	196
Callan McLean (9)	197
Riley Morrison	198
Max Hill (8)	199
Emily Robinson (9)	200
Benjamin Taylor (9)	201
Connor Savage (9)	202
Ava Hunter (9)	203
Arya Stark (8)	204
Keira Birrell (9)	205
Lauren Macdonald (9)	206
Freya Stephen (9)	207
Lauren Hill	208
Ellie Pearson (9)	209

The Stories

THE NEVER-ENDING FIGHT

'Dear enemies/rivals,

I'm writing to you to say that our last fight is not over yet and you will be punished harshly if you don't end this disgraceful fight.

As a celebrity, I now command you to stop this instant. So stop messing around!

Sincerely, Taylor Swift.'

"The great singer is commanding to make our lives miserable if we don't stop stealing her spotlight!"

"No, you shouldn't," she said as she took off her mask. "She is pure evil, she deserves it!"

"OMG, you were here all this time? Okay, but promise you'll help me."

"Promise!"

Part 2 coming soon...

Veronika Zlonkevych (10)

All Saints Benhilton CE Primary School, Sutton

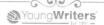

A TROPICAL DESTRUCTION

Beware! This page may cause destruction!
Terrrshhh! "Simon, get out of the way!" screamed
Greta as she smashed the ginormous, hairy palm
tree on the unknown monster, knocking both her
beloved friend and the muscular monster down.
"Noooo!" she cried as she desperately tried to save
him. But at that exact moment in time, the
monster threw the palm tree up into the air.
The terrifying monster of the tropical lands
stomped over to Greta as loudly as possible,
shaking all the lands around.
Greta opened her mouth and cried, "Be gone!"
Neither of them were ever found!

Stevie Smith (10)
All Saints Benhilton CE Primary School, Sutton

SOFIA AND HER ADVENTURE

Sofia cried that night. She thought she'd never feel happy again. Why was her life this way? Her horrid mother had locked her up in this great tower and now she was stuck.

"Shut it!" screeched her mother through the old, dusty shutter. The shutter, how could she have not realised? Slowly but surely, Sofia crawled through the shutter. She fell down, down, down. Then, she landed in a soft, cotton-like bush... but it wasn't a bush, it was a *dog!*

Sheran like never before. Sofia reached a dock. Sofia sailed away and lived happily on the sea.

Layla Bradley (10)
All Saints Benhilton CE Primary School, Sutton

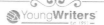
TRAPPED IN THE WAR ZONE

April 9th 2022, a day like any other day. I was flicking through the television channels in search of an interesting programme. I stumbled across the news. Then without further warning, the deafening sound of missiles and bombs being dispatched filled my ears.

The smell of burning buildings filled my nostrils. I watched from my window in horror as smoke filled the air. Families were running helter-skelter looking for refuge. *War is looming*, I thought to myself.

I prayed that this was all a daydream and not reality. That's when I knew war was heading my way - with no mercy.

Joanna Idowu (11)

All Saints Benhilton CE Primary School, Sutton

THE FOOTBALL PLAYER

Once there was a boy called Tom and he was an extraordinary, mind-blowing football player. He supported Tottenham and played for a football club in the Morden Little League. He'd *never* won a football match because of his terrible, appalling teammates.

Next week, he had a football match and tried as best as he could... but he lost! Tom was so angry, it felt like he could melt at any minute. He went home angrily.

The next day, he played *another* football match and tried really hard... And he finally won! He was so happy, it brightened up his day!

Jasper Tyler (9)
All Saints Benhilton CE Primary School, Sutton

A TWIST IN THE VOID

I know what you're thinking. You think that this story is going to be like one of those Disney movies with all the pretty princesses and the princes and stuff like that. But guess what, it's not! So now I'll make you suffer for your own choices. This story is about a void. Not just any ordinary void, it's mind-controlling and significantly threatening. It will kill you. The void kills cute, fascinating children, including kids like Anastacia, Grenon and Sophia. They were all at school until they went outside and saw this thing, but they didn't know what it was.

Keera Bates (11)
All Saints Benhilton CE Primary School, Sutton

THE MISERABLE HOUSE

One sunny morning, the sun was shining brightly on a hill that had one special house on it... Wonder why I'm saying 'special'? Well, carry on reading and you'll find out. This house was a very joyful house on the outside. But on the inside, it was a completely different story. On the inside, it was miserable and sad. Do you know why it was sad? Well, here's why. There used to be an old lady who lived there but she didn't really care about life. Every time a child came up the hill, there would be a complaint.

Renee-Lou Williams (10)
All Saints Benhilton CE Primary School, Sutton

THE GIRL WHO HAD HALLUCINATIONS

A story based on hallucinations and love

One Friday morning, a girl called Frances was walking to school when she started to get a headache. As she continued walking, she had a massive panic attack and then she fainted. She fell unconscious. She started to regain consciousness and then she started to see a familiar face. The face was attractive with dirty blonde hair and beautiful blue eyes. It was Jacob, the hottest boy in the class. As he carried Frances into school, they stared at each other and then... they leaned in for a kiss. But would their love last forever?

Queenie Kyere (9)
All Saints Benhilton CE Primary School, Sutton

I SAW A STATUE THAT CHANGED MY LIFE

One day, as I was doing my homework, I realised my cousins were coming over. I remembered how we were planning to see a cave with a statue of a snake lady. Apparently, if you looked her in the eyes, you turned into a statue.

A while after I finished my homework, I heard a knock. Knowing it was my cousins, I rushed to my front door and let them in. We packed food in case we got hungry.

When we got there, I suddenly heard one of my cousins scream, "Help!" We rushed over and saw... "Arghhh! She-"

Sahana Suthakaran (10)

All Saints Benhilton CE Primary School, Sutton

THE SHADOWY FIGURE

Once there was a little girl called Ava. She was really nice. She didn't have a nice family, so one afternoon, she escaped the dark, gloomy house and moved into a cave in the woods. She was so scared, she moved to the darkest corner of the cave. Then she noticed that she'd forgotten to bring delicious food, so she went to a nearby berry bush. She didn't like the feeling of being alone as she was only seven. She wanted to go back home. When she was trying to find her way out, she saw a shadowy figure...

Amber Chapman (9)

All Saints Benhilton CE Primary School, Sutton

FOOTBALL

One day, I was at the park when I saw a group of people playing football, so I asked them if I could play. They said, "Okay."
I started to play, but as I was so bad, I fell down and lost the game. After they left, I felt very sad because they laughed at me. I saw a man practising football, so I asked if he could coach me. He said, "Yes."
The next morning, I woke up very early and sprinted to the park. We started to train day after day. Later, I played against them and won.

Ansam Abdlfaddeel (9)
All Saints Benhilton CE Primary School, Sutton

DIARY OF FEELINGS

Hello! My name is Shane. Do you ever wonder what it feels like to be as angry as a storm? Well, I do because most of the time, I am angry. Most of the time, I feel angry because people just push in the line at school. It's not right and it's not fair! When I actually feel happy at school it's when we actually get through a lesson. But that is impossible because my class are the noisiest in the whole school! The only time I have been sad is: Never! Well, I'm out of pages, so bye!

Shane Navaratnarajah (10)

All Saints Benhilton CE Primary School, Sutton

THE FAIRY AND THE GOBLIN

Once upon a time, there was a fairy and living near that fairy was an evil goblin. The goblin hated all the fairies. So one day, the goblin went up to hurt the fairy. But just then, the fairy noticed and magicked the evil goblin away.

Joshua Cockburn (8)
All Saints Benhilton CE Primary School, Sutton

ORANGE MONKEY

One sunny morning, a bright orange monkey strolled through the bright, green, quiet forest. Sophia Puzzle had lost her mum!

"Hush, little monkey, don't you cry. I'll help you find her," said the butterfly. "Let's have a think. How big is she?"

"Big," said Sophia. "Bigger than me, bigger than you."

"Then I've seen your mum, come, little monkey, come."

"No, no, no, that's an elephant! My mum isn't a great grey hunk, she doesn't have a trunk! Anyway, her tail coils around trees."

"She must be near then."

Looking round and round, then up in the trees, they saw...

Sophia Athersmith (8)

Barlaston First School, Barlaston

THE WOODLOUSE

A Gruffalo took a stroll through the deep, dark wood. A chicken saw the Gruffalo and the Gruffalo looked good.

"Where are you going to big, brown Gruffalo? Come and have tea in my amazing wooden house."

"That's terribly kind of you, Chicken, but no, I'm going to have tea with a mouse."

"A mouse, scary! Bye-bye. I'd like to see you again."

Next, the Gruffalo saw a woodlouse and the woodlouse said, "Hi, Gruffalo. Do you want some lunch?"

"No thanks, I'm having tea with a mouse."

"But I have room."

"Oh, okay."

The woodlouse was very, very hungry.

Sophie Plant (8)
Barlaston First School, Barlaston

ORANGE AND THE MONSTER

One sunny afternoon, Orange was in her golden palace when suddenly, she heard a strange noise. It sounded like chalk scraping on a blackboard. There was the banging of cupboard doors, and in amongst all those horrible noises, she could hear eerie voices. It was coming from Ruby's backyard. "Ruby!" yelled Orange.

But just then, she heard a familiar voice.

"Ruby?" I whispered, "Is that you? What happened to you?"

She'd changed. She looked different. Orange ran. "Crystal, Emerald, Pearl! Come quickly, the monster is back. It's got hold of Ruby, come on!"

Olivia Ayre (8)
Barlaston First School, Barlaston

LEO'S NOT SO ORDINARY DAY

One ordinary day, Leo was playing football when he heard a bang. He looked but nothing was there. He checked again and spotted tiny floating creatures. He screamed with excitement. Suddenly, a fully grown wolf dashed through Leo's door. Leo threw a right hook to the ribs of the wolf. The floating creatures struck lightning to its heart so powerfully that its organs spread like viruses! No sooner than Leo had cleaned up, aliens attacked. Leo threw a punch and it killed one alien. The floating creatures killed five more. Leo shrieked with laughter because the creatures had helped him.

Rhys Whalley (8)
Barlaston First School, Barlaston

GRANDMA FIGHTS BACK

Once upon a time, a little girl was walking in the forest when she heard the trees whispering to her, "Be careful, the wolf is coming!"

In her basket were cakes, berries and biscuits for Grandma. She heard a twig snap behind her. She looked around and saw nothing.

Before long, she was at Grandma's cottage. She went inside and saw the wolf in Grandma's bed. She shook with fear.

A rattle came from the wardrobe. Suddenly, Ninja Grandma busted out!

I won't give you all the details, but let's just say Grandma and Red had something tasty for dinner!

Solomon Johnson (8)

Barlaston First School, Barlaston

ME AND THE WORMS

I was just drifting off to sleep when I saw three worms wriggling by. They were wriggling so fast that it made me want to follow them. They spotted me and tried to hide. I searched and eventually found them. They wriggled away into their house, which was surprisingly large.

"Let me in," I called.

"No!" said the worms, "You will eat us!"

"Why would I do that? I just want to be your friend," I said.

For some reason, they didn't believe me. So I flapped my feathers and flew away! The worms lived happily ever after.

Oliver Bloor (8)
Barlaston First School, Barlaston

THE MYSTERY OF MRS BROOM

One boring afternoon, I walked into Mrs Broom's class and noticed that Mrs Broom looked a little different. Her clothes were all black and her usually blue eyes had turned pale green.

Our first lesson was science. I felt nervous as there were potions everywhere. After everyone had hopped into their seats, Mrs Broom began teaching. She started a potion to turn us all into fish. I realised what was happening, so I threw a potion at her and she started shrinking.

Luckily, I trapped her in the empty potion jar. Worryingly, our new teacher was called Mr Wolf!

Elsie Harper (8)
Barlaston First School, Barlaston

HANSEL AND GRETEL

Hansel and Gretel found a witch's house. They knocked on the door. The witch said, "Come in - have all the sweets you want, come here!"
So they entered. It was creepy! Hansel almost left, he really should have followed his instincts! It was an old, crusty, musty house but it smelt brilliant! The witch had lured them into a trap.
Instantly, they were in the process of being cooked to death! The witch ate them in a flash!
Hansel and Gretel's parents looked and looked for them, but eventually gave up. No one lived happily ever after.

Rohan Sherratt (8)
Barlaston First School, Barlaston

THE TITANIC SAVIOUR

It was 10th April 1912, Captain Smith was loading people onto The Titanic ready to set sail into the dark, navy blue Atlantic Ocean. It all seemed to be going quite well until... a colossal iceberg got in the way!

Inconveniently, Captain Smith was on his lunch. Everyone was screaming at the top of their lungs. Just then, a young man named Cole sprung from his seat. Rushing towards the ship's wheel, he heaved it round - rapidly steering the ship to safety.

Everyone turned to face their saviour and started to clap as loud as thunder. He was a hero.

Hetti Warrington (8)
Barlaston First School, Barlaston

SPECIAL CHECKOUT

One dark evening, Stewart was shopping when he bought some fruit. He needed to pay, but there wasn't a checkout. In the shop, someone said to go through the wall to get to the special checkout. Stewart nervously went through.

After he'd paid, he looked around and saw a potion school, it looked amazing! He looked at some of the potions and decided to try one. He drank it all and *pop!* He turned small. So small, nobody could see him. He was angry, so looked around for another potion. Luckily, he found one that said 'Big' on the side.

Jonah Shooter (8)
Barlaston First School, Barlaston

CAVE BABY

Cave Baby was playing one evening. Suddenly, there was a gigantic stomp. Cave Baby was frightened. He didn't understand. Luckily, it was just his dad checking on him!

At bedtime, he fell asleep. He was woken by a furry animal brushing their skin on his face. Luckily, it was just his mum's hair as she kissed him goodnight.

Later, a sound woke him up. It sounded like a ghost wailing. Luckily, it was just an owl hooting outside.

Eventually, the sun came up and Mum and Dad came to get him from his cot. What an eventful and exhausting night!

Keira Bott (8)
Barlaston First School, Barlaston

LITTLE RED RIDING HOOD

Once upon a time, there was a girl called Little Red Riding Hood. She was dancing along Rebus Road with a basket of cupcakes that Mum had asked her to take to Grandma's. Grandma lived in a little cottage on a hill. Red Riding Hood was happily climbing the hill as she loved the view.

When she arrived at her grandma's, she opened the door and noticed Grandma in bed.

"Come closer," called Grandma.

It wasn't Grandma! It was a wolf in disguise. Red Riding Hood kicked the wolf so hard that he ran away and was never seen again!

Alfie Pitchfork (9)

Barlaston First School, Barlaston

THE PIG AND THE THREE LITTLE WOLVES

Once upon a time, there was a pig who was really lonely. He wanted to make friends with the three little wolves but the wolves' mother said, "Don't trust that pig!"

So the pig tried to think of a plan to get the wolves to be his friends. Eventually, he came up with the perfect plan. He would destroy their homes and offer them rooms in his house.

He smashed their houses down with his sledgehammer and then shouted, "Come and live with me!" Unsurprisingly, the wolves refused.

Now, the pig was tired, angry and lonely!

Joseph Peck (8)
Barlaston First School, Barlaston

THE GIRL AND THE WOLVES

There was a little girl who knew two wolves that lived in the woods. One day, she met one wolf walking through the woods.

The wolf said, "There's another wolf going to your dad's house to eat you both up!"

The little girl agreed that the good wolf could come to her house to help them.

When they got there, the little girl sneaked in and collected some boiling water. They both hid and waited for the bad wolf.

Once they saw him, they threw the boiling water at him. He ran off howling! Luckily, they never saw him again.

Connie Johnston (8)

Barlaston First School, Barlaston

THE TRUE TALE OF GOLDILOCKS AND THE THREE BEARS

Once upon a time in an enchanted forest, there lived three little bears and one small human with her mother. Unfortunately, the bears didn't like them, so the bears set out on a mission to get them away from the forest.

While Goldilocks and her mother were out collecting berries, the bears went into their house and trashed it. Every dish, every mug, every plate. Everything was broken into pieces.

When Goldilocks found out, she was devastated. They had to move to a new apartment. Eventually, she got her revenge by eating all their porridge!

Florence Fitzgerald (9)
Barlaston First School, Barlaston

LAPLAND

Once there were three little huskies called Dave, Max and Simba. They all went into the woods and were emoting, dabbing and flexing their money! Then a crow swooped down and scared them. That little bird had the guts to attack them.

Dave found some snow and made a house. The crow tapped the house down.

Max built a shelter in the trees. The crow jumped on the branches and shook the shelter down.

Simba built a house with ice blocks. The huskies hid in the house and eventually, the crow flew away. The huskies lived happily ever after.

Oliver Mottram (8)

Barlaston First School, Barlaston

THE WASHING MACHINE

One dark afternoon, Liv, the youngest girl, was bored doing nothing. So she did her chores. The first thing Liv wanted to do was the washing, but she needed help, so she called Sophie.

Liv yelled, "Sophie!"

Sophie came reluctantly, she couldn't ignore her after all. Sophie got bored, so she left. Liv sighed, but in the blink of an eye, she got sucked into the washing machine! She thought that she was doomed, when all of a sudden, she saw an old birch tree. It gave her a strange feeling, but she knew everything would be okay.

Isabelle Underwood (8)

Barlaston First School, Barlaston

THE MISSING STAR

One winter morning, there was a girl elf called Tinsel and a boy elf called Ben. They flew through the snow, but when they saw the Christmas tree, the star was missing! Tinsel told Santa about the missing star. "Oh no!" shouted Santa.
Then they looked up and down, but they couldn't find it. Then they went on Santa's sleigh but there was only Rudolph left to help them.
Ben said, "All I want to do is fly."
So off Rudolph went. Tinsel grabbed the chain and at the end of it, she saw... the missing star!

Charlotte Hackney (8)
Barlaston First School, Barlaston

THE TRUTH ABOUT THE TITANIC

On one stormy night in 1912, Captain Dan was sailing his ship, The Titanic, across the cold, dark Atlantic Ocean. He began to hear a strange whistling sound. It gradually got louder and louder. Suddenly, a meteorite crashed into the boat.

The passengers crammed onto the lifeboats and began drifting out into the ocean. Unfortunately, some lifeboats were popped by passing sharks! A killer whale smashed into another few. Eventually, two lonely lifeboats made it to shore. The survivors vowed never to tell the truth about the tale... until now!

Joshua Harding (8)

Barlaston First School, Barlaston

CUTDOWN

One sunny day, William was in the forest. William was excited because he was going to his dad's house. There was a villain called Cutdown who went around chopping down all of the trees.

One day, he fell down hard while chopping down an oak and slipped into a well. He woke up in a magical world but hated it. He tried so hard to escape, but couldn't get out of the well.

One long year later, he managed to escape. William saw him in the forest and ran home to his dad. "Don't worry, William. It's time for bed."

Sebastian Abbott (7)
Barlaston First School, Barlaston

MEAN GRINCH

One Snowy morning, there was a green, furry Grinch and he strolled through the freezing cold snow. The Grinch ruined Christmas and took all of the presents from under the Christmas trees. He also took all of the Christmas lights in the whole town so there wouldn't be another Christmas ever again. Next, he found a girl called Cindy Lou and put her down a wrapping machine. She came out the other side wrapped in paper.

Luckily, her dad turned up to find that she was alright. They watched the mean Grinch as he was scared out of town.

Imogen Rowson (7)
Barlaston First School, Barlaston

THE WOLF AND THE PIGS

Once upon a time, three bad pigs lived in the woods. One of the pigs chopped down a tree but it fell on him.

A wolf came along and asked, "Do you need any help?"

"No," said the pig stubbornly.

Eventually, he escaped. The three pigs chased the wolf back to his straw house. The pigs blew the house down. They chased the wolf until he hid in a stick house. Again, they blew the house down. He ran to a brick house that the pigs couldn't blow down. They got bored and went away. He lived happily ever after.

Finlay Burrow (8)
Barlaston First School, Barlaston

JACK AND THE BEANS - TALK

One day, Jack was walking across his lawn when he found a pile of fresh beans lying on the grass. Suddenly, they magically spoke to Jack. They said that the troll was going to come and defeat Jack and take all of his riches, including the goose that laid the golden eggs.

The beans told Jack to brew a fight potion. Jack drank the potion and felt fearless. He quickly rushed to the armoury and bought a magic shining sword and some shimmering armour.

Jack defeated the troll with one swoosh of his sword and kept all of his riches.

Frida Holm Mather (8)
Barlaston First School, Barlaston

JACK'S TALE

In the town of Costock, a boy called Jack was so poor, he stole to stay alive. One day, he stole an apple from a stall. The market seller was very angry and chased Jack to the river where he hopped onto a barge.

From daylight to darkness, he was on the boat. Unfortunately, a waterfall appeared. At the bottom, the barge broke. Jack swam to shore and found himself in a place where the houses were black and white and the people wore very bright clothes. However, Jack found he didn't need money, so he could live there happily.

Elijah Bryan (9)
Barlaston First School, Barlaston

THE TRUTH ABOUT ME

I was strolling around my beloved garden when I saw three little wolves wandering around. I followed them, but they ran away.

I tried to spot them, but they were too quick. I kept on walking and came across them in a house.

I tried to blow it down to get them out, but they just ran to the next house. I tried again. You can guess what happened!

I tried one final time. I lost my breath, so scrambled onto the roof to shout down the chimney. Unfortunately, I ended up in their dinner pot. Just a little misunderstanding!

Benjamin Hollingshurst (8)
Barlaston First School, Barlaston

LAUREN AND THE LEMON TREE

Once there was a little girl called Lauren.
One day, she was picking lemons from her freshly grown lemon tree. But one sunny afternoon, she saw the fattest, juiciest lemon of all. Sadly, it was at the top of the tree. She thought to herself that it was worth the risk, so she climbed. The tree seemed to never end. She reached the gigantic lemon. Just as she reached for it, she heard the sound of a thousand voices ringing in her ears. She scrambled down the lemon tree and saw something moving in the bushes... She ran.

Lauren Brown (8)
Barlaston First School, Barlaston

THE FOX HUNT

Frosty the fox lived in the woods. People hated Frosty because he ate their pets. They sent hunters to get him.

Frosty heard the hunters, so he hid. He was super scared. He ran and ran and ran until he was out of breath. He was safely hidden in a bush.

Soon, he spotted a rabbit and couldn't help himself - he ate it! The hunters spotted him and chased him right out of the woods.

He saw a human about to fall off a bridge. He leapt and grabbed them in his jaws! He saved her. Then everyone liked him.

Samuel Carr (8)
Barlaston First School, Barlaston

THE GIANT AND JACK

I was eating my dinner when a tiny boy popped up from the ground. Suddenly, the boy was in my house peeking at all my precious money.

I shouted, "Stop!" But he just came running out with my glorious, glistening crown. I went rushing after the boy down the spiral staircase.

We finally got to the bottom and the boy came rushing out from his house with an axe and fiercely chopped the staircase down. I had to build a new set of stairs! It was a very long walk back home without even finding my crown.

Daniel Harding (8)

Barlaston First School, Barlaston

POLAR EXPRESS

One sunny morning, there was a little girl called Susan. She got on the Polar Express and she was so happy. She sat down and had delicious hot chocolate on her way to the North Pole. She was excited to see Santa. Suddenly, he appeared! Santa asked if Susan could help him do a huge job. She had to ride on the sleigh and help him deliver all of the presents to the children. Santa was so proud of Susan, he thanked her and gave her the final present. She reappeared back on the Polar Express. She was going home.

Emma Bourne (7)
Barlaston First School, Barlaston

THE CASTLE AND THE TIGER

Once upon a time in a sunny forest, Rowan found a strange cupboard. He opened it and got sucked in! Suddenly, he found an odd castle. Opposite the castle was a wood. Rowan decided to go in. When he got there, he saw two of his friends playing tag in the woods. Rowan tried to say hello but they were too busy playing tag. Suddenly, a magical tiger came by and set up a campfire. They all toasted marshmallows together and the boys fell asleep. Rowan quickly dreamt of home. Suddenly, he was back there.

William Brough (7)

Barlaston First School, Barlaston

BEAUTY AND THE BEAST: THE PROLOGUE

One day, I was happily strolling through my castle, when all of a sudden, my neighbour (who was a witch) strode up to me. Without warning, she zapped me with her wand.

Before I knew it, I grew a tail and fur replaced my skin. I thought that I would never feel the same. Imagine spending all your days as a beast! How would I ever become human again?

I needed someone to see me for who I really was. I waited and waited and waited until one day, a merchant came wandering into my castle gardens...

Dylan Graham (8)
Barlaston First School, Barlaston

THE CAVE

One damp day, Bob found a cave. He had no home and he was cold, so he went into the cave to bed. It was rocky, gross and horrible. He went to sleep and dreamt of Christmas. He decided to sneak into Christmas Land to try and steal Christmas because he felt so sad. He slowly went to the houses and stole the presents and toys. Suddenly, Bob's dog, Banana, appeared. He had a magical tool on his back to steal Christmas lights.

He got back to the cave, but he felt so bad, he gave it all back.

Isaac Graham (7)

Barlaston First School, Barlaston

SISTER MYSTERY

It's a sunny morning, I go to my sister's room. It's empty! I shout her name... no reply. I look around, she's gone.

Days pass, I finally find her but she isn't her normal self. She wants to hurt me. Suddenly, I smell a sweet, sickly smell and I faint.

The next thing I know, my sister dumps me in the sea. I float, semi-conscious. A boat comes and saves me. When I eventually get home, my sister gets taken away. We never discovered what happened to twist her so much.

Lyla Whalley (8)
Barlaston First School, Barlaston

CAN'T YOU SLEEP, DOTTY?

Dotty was trying to get to sleep, but she couldn't. So he asked his friend, the bird, who said he should have a drink. It didn't work, so he went to the cat instead. The cat said, "Get a teddy!"
It didn't work, so he went to the tortoise. He said to find a friend and have a cuddle, so he did. Then he realised why he couldn't sleep. It was actually daytime the whole time. Dotty the puppy had been working so hard that he had tried to sleep through the day.

Willow Abbott (7)

Barlaston First School, Barlaston

LILY AND THE ACORN TREE

Once upon a time, a girl named Lily was walking through the woods. She saw a bean on the floor. She took the bean home. Her mum was furious and threw them outside.

The next morning, Lily saw a big acorn tree. She climbed and climbed. She saw a castle and went inside to find a bag of diamonds. They were rich! Suddenly, the giant came down the acorn tree. The giant ate Lily but somehow turned into Lily. The giant ruled the forest and lived badly ever after, feeling sadness for Lily forever.

Freya Kemp (7)

Barlaston First School, Barlaston

SNOW WHITE

When Snow White was banished from the castle, it was really a plan to save her.

After walking in the forest for days, Snow White came across a tiny cottage. The dwarves inside seemed friendly, but really, they had a cunning plan! They made her a poison apple pie. Snow White was just about to try it when there was a knock at the door. It was the good queen.

"Run!" she shouted.

Snow White and the queen ran back to the castle. They lived happily ever after.

Aaliyah Constable (8)

Barlaston First School, Barlaston

SAMMY

One damp afternoon, Sammy the Cocker Spaniel saw a mysterious creature in the woods. He realised it was a German shepherd. He ran to play with it but accidentally fell through a portal into Dog Land. He sniffed around and was very curious. He found food, treats and toys to play with. Suddenly, an evil monster came along and tried to push Sammy into a bog to trap him. Sammy bounced up and hit the monster quickly on the head. Nobody ever saw or heard about the monster ever again.

Isabel McPherson (8)
Barlaston First School, Barlaston

THE ELF

In a hotel, there was an elf called Henson. He climbed into a sack and by the time he climbed out, he was in Football Land. It was so fun. He saw that Football Land was filled with all of his favourite players, he couldn't believe it. He wanted to be a footballer so badly. Suddenly, the king of the footballers appeared. Henson asked if he could stay forever. The king said maybe one day, but today he needed to go home to his dad who would be worried.

Oliver Williams (7)
Barlaston First School, Barlaston

OVER THE OTHER SIDE OF THE SWING...

"Bet you can't swing all the way around!" my friend, Martin, yelled, laughing beside me.
I pushed forward on the swing. Air rippled all around me. I could feel excitement flooding through my body as I span.
Suddenly, I squealed as my stomach flipped and a curious feeling engulfed my body. I came to a stop, gasping for air. "Woah," I breathed.
Peering to my left I saw... myself! A gasp that sounded nothing like my voice burst out. It was a man's voice. A man's voice I knew...
My stomach plummeted with fear as I realised... I was Martin!

Parker Spence (7)
Cop Lane CE Primary School, Penwortham

DRAGON APPROACHING...

Its wings covered the sun. Its terrifying teeth were coming closer and closer. I gulped and my heart raced. A dragon! Its piercing eyes loomed towards me. Its feet slammed and shook the Earth. The grass tore apart beneath its claws. Smoke burst out of the horrifying beast. A breath gasped sharply against my throat.

It crouched down to glare at me. I trembled with fear, squeezing my eyes shut... I was going to die. Then slobber licked my body. My eyes widened in disbelief and I let out a laugh of relief as it wagged its ginormous horned tail!

Kaine Wilkinson (8)

Cop Lane CE Primary School, Penwortham

THE FOOTBALL DANCER

"Archie! Archie!" The crowd chanted my name. My eyes travelled to the goalkeeper and I gave him a smirk. The pressure pressed on my bones and my lungs were screaming. My heart was beating as fast as it could. I exhaled, letting out the nerves as the goalkeeper dripped with sweat, gulping. There was only one way to get past the wall of players. I knew what I had to do.

Raising my arms and lifting my leg, I launched into a pirouette! The wall scattered, confused. That's when I back-heeled the ball and it soared... Right into the goal.

Archie Taylor (8)

Cop Lane CE Primary School, Penwortham

WING ATTACK!

Chanting my name, the crowd clapped. Excitement exploded through my body. Dribbling the ball towards the net, a shadow loomed. Annoyance grew, the shadow was blocking the goal! Its eyes glared into mine, but then I heard my name being shouted and bravery swelled. I knew... it was time to fly!

Stretching my arms out wide, the dark red wings erupted and took me into the sky. Holding the ball against my football boot, I volleyed it and it zoomed... right into the net! I landed with a smirk and tucked my wings away as the crowd roared my name.

Henry Boyes (7)
Cop Lane CE Primary School, Penwortham

SCARY BERRY

John and his friends woke up.

"What the heck?" said John, "This isn't my house!"

"Let's explore!" said everyone.

"Arghhh! It's a ghost!"

"Hi, I'm dead," said the ghost.

"Hi?" said everyone, confused.

It crept up behind them.

"Do you know fish use gills to breathe?"

"Wow! Thanks," said the guys.

"I'm also gonna kill you!"

"Ha, what?" said John.

"Run!" Viktor added.

They ran out of the town, but when they did, the town disappeared.

"What the...?" *Dun, dun, dun!*

The killer was still there. He jump scared them.

"Ogga bogga bogga!"

"Arghhh!" they screamed.

They ran home. *Phew!*

Nathan Glynn (11)
Crawforddyke Primary School, Carluke

THE STRANGER WHO I THOUGHT WAS MY IDOL

Bang! "What was that?" Ellie said.

Ellie ran outside. There was nobody there. Ellie kept hearing big bangs inside the house next to her. Someone walked out of the house next to her. Ellie said, "Wait, is that Katy Perry?"

She didn't mind though. Then she heard Katy Perry's voice.

Ellie said, "No way, that's my favourite singer!"

Ellie ran out and said hi, but it was a stranger. Then Ellie thought, *but their voice is like Katy Perry's*. The person came to the door and said, "Bla, bla, bla!"

Ellie then said, "You're an alien! Someone, please help me!"

Sophia Thomson (11)

Crawforddyke Primary School, Carluke

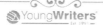

THE ANGRY ALIENS

"Meteorite!" Captain tried to turn.

"I can't turn, we are going to crash!" he shouted.

Crash! "Are they aliens? They've got a gun! Run!"
The spaceship fell into the ocean and the alien ship
chased them. The aliens stole the lifeboats needed
to save everyone. Captain noticed a huge whale
and thought the whale could help them.

Everyone jumped on the whale. Suddenly, the
whale swam towards the aliens.

"Why is the whale turning? Nooo!"

He was a spy whale! Everyone jumped off the
whale and swam for freedom! "Hooray!"

They escaped from the aliens and made it home!

Ella Smith (10)
Crawforddyke Primary School, Carluke

A TIME-TRAVELLING TWIST

"We're one lightyear away," said the smart ship.
"Finally, we're safe from those space asteroids."
One hour later, Willow said, "We're here!"
Jack and Willow had crashlanded in Asda.
"What is this place?" asked Jack.
"It's the place where people go shopping."
"We haven't got time for that!" moaned Jack.
Little did Jack know, Willow was communicating with someone. Jack ran out to find the parts of the crashed ship. But then as he turned around, he saw a giant party from the past and future wishing him a happy birthday. Was it a trick?

Aarush Santapur (11)
Crawforddyke Primary School, Carluke

THE BATTLE OF THE CHANNEL

"Go quick, Colonel Smith. Go and infiltrate the ship! Lieutenant Winggrove, setup artillery!" shouted Rodger. "Sergeant Billy, go with Colonel Smith. Take some guns."

"Okay Sir, I'll go."

"The Nazis won't stop firing! I don't know what to do, Sir!"

Meanwhile, Colonel Smith snuck on the destroyer and Sergeant Billy came with him. On the boat, Colonel Smith took out a guard and shot the captain.

Meanwhile, at the base, a British destroyer entered the Channel and destroyed a German ship. Colonel Smith was on the ship and it sank. It turned out Sergeant Billy was a German spy!

Ewan Rodger (10)
Crawforddyke Primary School, Carluke

THE CREEPY NEIGHBOUR

Saffron's neighbour, Ethan, seemed extremely creepy and dangerous. It often looked like he was carrying a gun! Saffron was really suspicious, so she'd watch her neighbour every day.

One day, Saffron watched Ethan carry what looked like body bags into his house. Saffron felt brave and decided to confront Ethan.

She asked, "Why do you have a gun, and why do you bring body bags into your house every day?" Ethan laughed. "What? This? This is my walking stick! Those aren't body bags either, they're money bags! I'm a billionaire!"

Saffron was so surprised. She had got it all wrong!

Cara-Violet Tait (10)
Crawforddyke Primary School, Carluke

THE GIRL AND THE FOREST

Walking further into the screaming forest, "Oh no, I'm lost!" she said, taking a couple of steps. "I don't feel good." She sat down to rest. Her vision slowly became blurry, then everything went black.
Later, she woke up in a strange place.
"Where am I?" she said, looking around at lovely blossom trees and wild flowers. Wandering around, she saw a herd of unicorns, but they galloped away before she could get close. Wandering for a little longer, she realised she wasn't getting out.
"At least I'm in a beautiful place."
That was 5 years ago. She's still missing.

Chloe Tough (11)
Crawforddyke Primary School, Carluke

THE CREATURE

"Father!" Duncan shouted.

He'd found a pattern engraved into the ship's walls. John sprinted over to take a closer look. "It says that the ship was built in 1349!" Duncan exclaimed, "400 years ago."

Suddenly, a crew member shouted down that there was a large rock, so John had to turn the ship. Duncan thought that the marks on the rock were fascinating. But... it moved?

The Rumbling Ramone, the most dangerous creature during the 1400s, appeared out of the water. John grabbed his sword as he stood on the edge of the ship and dived bravely into the ocean...

Ailsa McNeill (10)

Crawforddyke Primary School, Carluke

THE MAGICAL CARAVAN

One windy day, Emily and her class went on a walk through the town. Weirdly, they found something that they had never seen before. In the woods was an unusual caravan.

The teacher asked, "Who wants to look around it?" And everybody said, "Me!"

As they were walking around, they saw someone wearing all black. The teacher asked him what his name was and he replied, "Raven."

He took them all inside, but it was not as Emily expected. There was blood everywhere and half the floor was missing. Emily inspected further... It was a secret passageway to the future!

Lexie Glen (10)
Crawforddyke Primary School, Carluke

THE SCHOOL TRIP

"So today, class, we are going on a school trip," said Mrs Beans, "We're going to the zoo!"
The whole class jumped up and shouted, "Yeah!"
Mrs Beans said, "Calm down, we need to wait outside for the bus."
After one hour of waiting, the bus finally came.
Three hours later, they finally arrived at the zoo.
Mrs Beans said, "We are here."
She tried to open the door but they had been locked in the bus! They waited ages for the fire brigade to come and free them... and when they finally did, the zoo had closed!

Eve McLetchie (10)
Crawforddyke Primary School, Carluke

WORLD CUP FINAL MONSTERS

"Welcome to the World Cup final between Argentina and Portugal!"
The whistle blew and the game began. The match started like any other. Ronaldo had the ball, he shot and scored! The Argentina players were furious, but their manager had something up his sleeve. Suddenly, he pressed a button on his chair and the full place went into darkness.
Seconds later, the lights turned back on... Oh my! The whole Argentina squad had turned into monsters! The Portugal team tried their best to play but were too terrified! Goal after goal was scored by Argentina and victory was theirs!

Colton Clark (10)
Crawforddyke Primary School, Carluke

THE ADVENTURE OF BOB AND PIXEL BOY

"How?" said Bob.

Bob had been sucked into his TV screen and game. Bob met someone called Pixel Boy. Bob became great friends with Pixel Boy very easily.

"How do I get out?" asked Bob.

"You have to defeat the cave monster," said Pixel Boy.

They completed the levels and they were on the final level. The cave monster spat out rocks but they dodged them. They finally defeated the scary cave monster. Bob tried to leave but was still trapped! Bob was confused and scared. Pixel Boy had tricked him! Bob was really mad. He was stuck there forever!

Jamie Adams (10)
Crawforddyke Primary School, Carluke

THAT HALLOWEEN NIGHT!

One Halloween night, a group of five friends all went out trick or treating. They noticed everyone was acting a little strange. No one was out trick or treating, no one was answering the door. What was happening?

That night, it was a red moon. Then suddenly, everything went black. It was so dark. But then, "Arghhh!" They heard a scream in the distance. Everyone was wondering what had happened, but they all started hearing footsteps coming towards them. What was that? They were never seen again. Well, until now, I guess...

I'm one of the girls from that night!

Erin McLeod (11)

Crawforddyke Primary School, Carluke

THE GLORIOUS GOAL BY GAKPO

It was a sunny day in Qatar. Gakpo was about to start in the biggest game of his life. The game started and Gakpo was excited. Gakpo tried to score, but Alisson somehow saved it. Neymar whizzed past the Dutch defenders, but he missed his shot! The half-time whistle blew.

The second half started. Gakpo had control of the ball but Casemiro tackled him.

In the 90th minute, Gakpo finally scored. The Netherlands lifted the World Cup and they were the champions. Afterwards, the Netherlands found out that the Brazilian defenders were robots. Brazil was banned from the World Cup.

Reegan Muir (10)
Crawforddyke Primary School, Carluke

HALLOWEEN DREAM?

Issey was so excited to go to the Halloween Fair. She went with her friend, Sienna. They arrived and got food, then they went into the corn maze. It was very spooky, there were no lights at all. They began to run as they heard screams.

"Sienna, where are you?" said Issey.

She heard her friend scream and she ran towards a light. Sienna was standing at the light. It was a portal. They both ran through it...

Suddenly, Issey woke up in her bedroom.

"Wake up, Issey! Time for school!"

"What?"

It was all a dream, or was it?

Kacie Pratt (11)
Crawforddyke Primary School, Carluke

THE CLASS MONSTER

Billy went to school and was having a great time playing with his friends. Suddenly, the lights went out. It lasted for hours and Billy couldn't go anywhere because it was too dark.

Finally, the lights turned back on with a flicker. Everybody had disappeared! Little Billy didn't know what to do, he just stood there confused.

Suddenly, a cute monster appeared on Billy's seat. It jumped on Billy and bit him! Billy passed out. When he woke up, he felt different... The monster bite had changed him. Billy had become evil and everyone was in danger!

Chloe Gardiner (10)

Crawforddyke Primary School, Carluke

THE SCHOOL TRIP THAT WENT WRONG

Elliana went on a school trip to Five Sisters Zoo. But on the way there, the driver took a wrong turn... They ended up at an abandoned school. As they tried to leave, a random brick wall appeared out of nowhere. Everyone jumped out of the bus and banged on the brick wall.

Suddenly, a terrifying rat jumped out of the school and started chasing them. It was a robot rat named Rickey Rat! He repeated one thing over and over, "Do you want tea with me?"

The kids shouted, "No, Rickey!"

Thankfully, the wall disappeared and they all escaped.

Libby Wilson (9)

Crawforddyke Primary School, Carluke

THE HAUNTED HOUSE

Cora went to her friend's birthday party in a haunted house. There were clowns and witch decorations everywhere. She was so excited! Cora went in and instantly got goosebumps and felt a shiver up her spine. She started to explore with her friend until a shadow ran past. She looked around and her friend was gone. She looked back at the entrance, but it was gone too! Cora spun around and passed out.

Cora woke up with her friend screaming. She ran towards her and saw the shadow again.

"Hahaha! Got you!" shouted Nova.

It was a joke all along!

Brooke Mason (9)

Crawforddyke Primary School, Carluke

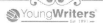

THE WOODS

Emily went to a boarding school. There was a mysterious wood, Emily had always wanted to explore the woods but she was always too scared. One day, she gained her confidence and went to the woods. Emily also had powers, she could turn into a wolf just in case anything happened.

She heard noises as she entered the woods. They were growing louder and louder. Emily could see a monster coming towards her, she started attacking it with her claws. It was too powerful. Emily was bleeding, she couldn't fight any longer. It got her. She was never... seen... again.

Jessica Davies (11)
Crawforddyke Primary School, Carluke

THE RED BUTTON

Noah came back from a long day at school. His mum told him they were moving away from the War Of Skeletons. They went to the cold underground city. He didn't ask any questions but he was suspicious.

The next day, he heard on TV that skeletons were invading the city. Some people from the underground got called up for the war.

When Noah was outside, he found a big red button which said: 'Only for professionals'. He thought it might destroy the city. He pressed it and waited a while. Initially, nothing happened... until he turned into a skeleton!

Hunter Naismith (10)

Crawforddyke Primary School, Carluke

THE LITTLE RED TWIST

Once upon a time, there was a little girl called May. May's grandma lived in a big forest that was mysterious.

One day, May's grandma was sick with a cold, so she wanted to take her some cookies. May set off to find Grandma's house.

Ten minutes later, she made it to her grandma's and went inside to see Grandma sleeping in the bed. May went over and gave her the cookies. Suddenly, there came a low growl and a wolf leapt in and gobbled up Grandma.

"And that's the story of how Grandma died," May said, 30 years later.

Eve Madden (11)
Crawforddyke Primary School, Carluke

THE SNEAKY MURDERER

George was on a small cruise of only ten people in the middle of the Pacific Ocean and there was a murderer amongst them! The first death was reported and the only thing you could hear were beating hearts and people praying to God. George was trying to stay away from everyone but one particular person continued to follow him... Was he the murderer? Death after death, the number of people continued to decrease. There were only three people left and they decided to separate. Another murder and now only two people left. One more... the murderer was George!

Ross Thomson (10)
Crawforddyke Primary School, Carluke

THE MONSTER

I was forced to join Twisted High. When I arrived, I met a girl called Alice, so I said, "Hi, I'm Friday." "I'm Alice," she said.

I couldn't be bothered talking, so I went to my happy place, the woods. I heard a scratch on the tree. I quickly turned around. It was Alice. All of a sudden, she changed into a werewolf! She chased me until the sun rose. It was starting to rise. I could feel my legs burning. Alice fell into a huge hole. I could feel my body burning.

"Help!" I screamed. There was no answer...

Jayden-James Mullen (11)
Crawforddyke Primary School, Carluke

SOPHIE'S VIDEO GAME ADVENTURE

Sophie was in school, daydreaming about a new video game. She was suddenly snapped out of her daydream by her teacher shouting her name. She got into trouble, but she didn't care. All she cared about was the new video game.

The school day ended and she rushed off to the arcade and started playing. The power went out and she felt a shock.

Sophie was in her favourite video game. She was pixelated too! She dodged, ducked and jumped through all the traps. The timer buzzed and Sophie jumped. She was back in class... She was dreaming all along!

Jessie Obinna (10)
Crawforddyke Primary School, Carluke

THE WIZARD NEXT DOOR

Dear Diary,
You will not believe what happened today! My neighbour, who I thought was ordinary, Mr Smith, turned out to be the most famous wizard in the world! Wacky Wizard Paul. You see, Wacky Wizard Paul is my idol. I have loved him for years and I always copy his magic tricks. Mr Smith thought no one would ever find out his secret identity, but I recognised that navy blue velvet waistcoat and his 'Magic Trick Association' medal immediately!
I'm super happy that I live next door to him... but I'll make sure to keep his secret!

Emma McCutcheon (9)
Crawforddyke Primary School, Carluke

THE GAS ATTACK

Carluke was in a time of danger. The warden had forgotten to sound the alarm. Gas was coming fast. The villagers were only realising this when the gas was metres away from killing them. Children ran as fast as possible, but oh no, they were about to get sucked into this mess. Everyone was walking around fine and all were breathing normally. The warden himself was shocked that gas never killed anyone. Turns out, it was only green fog. *Boom!* There was a bomb. Now, everyone was running faster than a racing car. Everyone was running to the shelters...

Grace Brown (11)
Crawforddyke Primary School, Carluke

EVIL ANIMALS

Once upon a time, there was a girl named Sia Macintosh. She loved going on school trips... and how lucky, she was going on a trip today to Aviemore woods!
As she went into the woods, everything seemed a little strange. The trees looked odd. Suspiciously looking around her, she went over to the tree. She fell into a hole and everything was red and black. She met some talking animals. They all seemed cute and cuddly, however, they were actually evil animals. They turned Sia into an animal too. She was a tiger. She ruled the animal kingdom forever!

Emma Paterson (10)
Crawforddyke Primary School, Carluke

THE MAGICAL HAMSTER

Hugo's family were going away for the day. While they were packing, Pickle the hamster was roaming around his cage.

As soon as they left home, Pickle transformed himself into a human. He went shopping for tasty human food, like pizza and chicken. Hugo forgot his phone and rushed back home. Pickle tried to clean up his mess and he jumped back into his cage... But he forgot about the pizza! Pickle had no choice but to transform back into a human and confess his superpower to the whole family. Hugo and Pickle became the best of friends!

Hugo Smith (10)
Crawforddyke Primary School, Carluke

JAMAR FROM AFAR

Jamar is a boy from Germany, so we think. He is a kid at Kane High School with one friend, Nicola. They have been friends since nursery. But Nicola didn't know about Jamar's evil side or his plan for the future. Jamar's plan was to take over the world with a mind-controlling gun built from materials never seen before because Jamar was from space! He dreamed about telling Nicola that he was from space, sharing the plan and taking over the world together, but he couldn't.

The next day, his plan was ready to take over the world.

Glen Cameron (11)
Crawforddyke Primary School, Carluke

THE FRIENDLY ALIENS

The astronaut had landed on the moon and was putting on his spacesuit before going on a moonwalk. Suddenly, an alien spaceship appeared from nowhere. The astronaut shivered in fear as he thought the aliens were going to hurt him. The astronaut started his spaceship to escape but he had no fuel. He hid in the spaceship and heard a bang on the door. The aliens were at the door. "We are friends!" they shouted. "Here is some fuel to get home."
The astronaut felt thankful and was relieved that the aliens had helped him.

Brodie Murdoch (10)
Crawforddyke Primary School, Carluke

EVELYN AND THE WOLF

One gloomy day, Evelyn went to a cafe. She sat at a table frustrated because her parents left her at a magic school. Her parents left her because she was using her magic too much and it was getting out of hand. Toby, the waiter, came over and served the food. Evelyn wasn't sure why, but she was suspicious of Toby.

Later that day, Evelyn followed Toby into the woods. She couldn't believe her eyes... Toby transformed into a wolf and attacked a lone hiker! Evelyn used her magic to throw Toby to the ground and she saved the hiker.

Ella Nisbet (10)
Crawforddyke Primary School, Carluke

NOVA'S WISH

There once was a nice girl called Nova and her mischievous friend, Kai. He often misbehaved but he could also be kind.

When Kai turned 30, he became Prime Minister of the UK. This was a bad idea. He told people to do silly things like putting toilet paper on houses and trees! He lost his job as Prime Minister and became Abbymoor's head teacher. Nova wasn't happy. She wanted to be the head teacher.

One day, Kai mistakenly set the school on fire! He was banned from the school and Nova got her wish. She became the head teacher.

Olivia Ferguson (10)
Crawforddyke Primary School, Carluke

SPACE MONSTER

I had just received a message from Neil saying that he was about to step on the moon. He stepped out and looked back at the rocket. It was floating into the darkness of space. He called back to me and explained what was happening.

I said, "Your safety cord will pull you back."

But then Neil said it had snapped. The signal started breaking up and before it fully cut off, he said, "They are watching me."

Then the signal fully cut off and Neil was never seen again. No one knows what happened to him after that.

Thomas Mooney (11)
Crawforddyke Primary School, Carluke

THE TIME TRAVELLER

Once upon a time, a wee while ago, a time traveller called Jamie was in the jungle looking for any creature or unusual things. He was just walking along with his magnifying glass and binoculars when all of a sudden, a baby raptor jumped out and tried to bite him.

Luckily, a person came out of nowhere and pushed him out of the way. She was an explorer called Elisabeth. They both introduced themselves.

But as that was happening, an indominus rex chased them. Fortunately, they escaped.

Sadly, they had to say goodbye and go home.

Macey Docherty (11)
Crawforddyke Primary School, Carluke

THE TWO FISHERMEN

Once upon a time, there were two brothers who were out fishing on a boat. Suddenly, an alien spaceship appeared and they felt scared. An alien floated towards them. He had a giant fishing rod, so he hooked them up into the ship. The boys were taken to the spaceship jail cell. They were locked in the cell for five long days. The aliens came back to the cell and took them to a large room filled with lots of wires. The aliens sent the brothers into another dimension! Unexpectedly, after two days, the aliens came back and saved them.

Bailey Leishman (9)
Crawforddyke Primary School, Carluke

THE STRANGE HOLIDAY

One strange holiday, Eva and Mark were at the pool bar. Eva spotted her mum coming towards them. She didn't say anything but her mum grabbed something from her bag and pointed it at them. The next thing they remember was a green portal opening. They woke up in a red world. They were confused. Mark was a green goblin! Eva freaked out. She was normal, unlike him. He tried to eat her head, but Eva grabbed a glass bottle from the floor with pink liquid in it and threw it at him. Thankfully, everything went back to normal again!

Ellie Laird (11)
Crawforddyke Primary School, Carluke

THE SNAIL ON THE ICE

Once there was an iceberg, his name was Mr Berg. He was a very lonely iceberg. He had nothing to do and he had no friends either... Until he met a snail named Jeffrey. They became best friends. Mr Berg was very happy that he was no longer lonely and the snail was delighted too. Suddenly, there was a boat coming straight towards Mr Berg! Mr Berg couldn't move! Jeffrey tried to help, but he couldn't move Mr Berg either. The boat crashed into Mr Berg and he broke into pieces! Jeffrey lost his friend but survived the crash.

Dominic Roddie (10)
Crawforddyke Primary School, Carluke

PERFECT PIGEON

Once upon a time, Pigeon and Patricia were walking to class when... Jerry attacked Patricia! Pigeon ran as fast as he could and told everybody to hide, but they didn't listen and they got attacked. Jerry ran out of the classroom, pulled an AK-47 out of his beak and shot Patricia. He ran out of class and realised all his classmates had turned into zombies! So he shot all of them down and ran out of school. He went home to see his human Pigepom sitting in his human bed. Pigeon told him to run and they escaped the zombies.

Eilidh Nicol (11)
Crawforddyke Primary School, Carluke

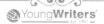

RILEY THE ROBOT

Riley the robot loved video games. He lost when he was playing his favourite game, FIFA, so he got angry and tried to break the TV. Suddenly, Riley got electrocuted and was turned into a human. Riley didn't realise this at first and continued acting like a robot. He sat down to eat his dinner of nuts and bolts but struggled to chew. He went to the mirror and was shocked to see that he was a human. Riley was really happy. He started doing more human things and ate human foods. Riley didn't want to be a robot again.

Riley Brady (10)
Crawforddyke Primary School, Carluke

THE MURDERER IN THE CLASS

Sitting in the class, like always, we were doing maths. There was a huge growl of thunder, so loud the building shook.

All of the lights in the school turned off and a man entered through the door. He was pointing a gun at us! We stopped what we were doing and tried to escape through the window.

But Bella was scared and she slipped. Her BFF laughed and left her. But luckily, another classmate saved her. Her BFF was left with the murderer, but it turned out she was one too and the murderer was her dad!

Kaitlyn Daly (10)
Crawforddyke Primary School, Carluke

THE UNEXPECTED EVENT

One day, Lucas was in school and the new girl sat next to him. She was very unusual, but Lucas didn't think anything of it. After break, she was annoying him. She kept tapping him.

After lunch, somebody broke into the school and held the new girl hostage. No one realised until Lucas went to the bathroom; the girl was locked inside. Lucas was waiting, the girl ran out. A man chased her and she slid to the floor. She suddenly pulled a pistol from her knickers and blasted him in the head... Lucas never saw her again!

Lucas Parker (11)

Crawforddyke Primary School, Carluke

THE MYSTERY MOUNTAIN

I was getting on the bus for our school trip. The bus set off on the adventure! I was so excited! One hour later, "We're nearly there!" shouted the driver. There was a mountain, we went up. The road was on a ledge with no barriers, it was very high up! We were going so fast, the driver hadn't noticed a bit of road had fallen off! I closed my eyes. I was so scared, I couldn't even think. But there was one thing I thought about; my family. After this day, the bus was never to be seen again...

Alea Fowler (11)

Crawforddyke Primary School, Carluke

JAKE AND DAISY

Once upon a time, there was a boy called Jake. He had a friend called Daisy who worked at the palace. Jake didn't know that Daisy had a crush on him. Jake had two evil stepbrothers who hated him and made him clean the house.

One day, the princess came and invited Jake round to the palace. When he got there, he saw Daisy and the princess. Then the princess asked Jake if he wanted to marry her tomorrow.

He said, "Yes!" Daisy was jealous.

At the wedding, right before the kiss, Jake ran out...

Charlotte Binnie (11)

Crawforddyke Primary School, Carluke

THE BIG MISTAKE

One day in Paris, Jullian and Owen were playing tag. They were running around and decided to go to the Eiffel Tower for a game there. It was about 6:30pm at night and very dark. They went to the top floor of the tower and Jullian started counting while Owen hid behind a box. Julian looked for Owen and suddenly, he jumped out from behind the box with a scream. Jullian quickly tagged him but too hard and Owen fell backwards. Owen flew through the air and off the top of the Eiffel Tower, never to be seen again...

Matthew Farmer (11)
Crawforddyke Primary School, Carluke

THE ALIEN ATTACK

I came home from school and I was playing my Xbox when a portal started forming behind me and a strange figure came out of it. Then it said, "Come with us, you're going to the alien prison." I said, "No!" and my brother heard me and came in. He saw the strange figure and turned into James Bond! He took the strange figure down. More kept coming, so we had to jump out of the window to escape quickly. We had to run as far as we could and I really wondered if I was an alien...

Rhoan Hendrie (11)
Crawforddyke Primary School, Carluke

SANDSTORM

Still in the desert, Eggy had no food and one half-filled water bottle. Eggy was hungry till a vending machine was seen in the distance. He ran and ran till he went through it and sand fell down where it was. Eggy was mad. He kicked the sand and it went in his eyes. He fell to the ground, screaming. He got the sand out of his eyes and looked around... "S-s-sandstorm!"

He ran the other way and kept running till he was in it. He got sand in his eyes and mouth. He woke in a dark, creepy room...

Jack Chapman (11)

Crawforddyke Primary School, Carluke

THE ID

One day, there was a boy called Jimmy. He was walking down the street when suddenly, a girl dropped her purse. He picked it up, but she had vanished onto a train. He'd just missed her. So he found her details on her ID and drove to her house and knocked on the door.

The girl answered the door. She thought that he was a robber and he'd taken her purse. So she killed him and dropped him off a cliff. She was happy that she had her purse back. His family heard he died and his family were sad.

Paige Babes (11)

Crawforddyke Primary School, Carluke

SUSPICIOUS SUMMER

One day, Summer moved to LA, but a weird part of LA. When they arrived, the house was weird and had a really weird neighbour. The neighbour never came out of his house. He blocked the windows so no light ever came in. He never let anyone in the house. Once, a girl went in and she was never seen again. Summer wanted to know if the girl ever got out. So Summer got a ladder and climbed through the window and found the girl - Millie. She was helping her to escape when she felt a hand on her back...

Anna Cruickshanks (11)
Crawforddyke Primary School, Carluke

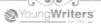

THE GAMER BOY

Leo the gamer loved playing Fall Guys. He was the best at the game but he got hacked. As he tried to fix the problem, he felt a huge electric shock! Leo suddenly felt something grabbing him by the leg... He noticed he was in the game! Leo had to be quick to complete the level, but he kept on falling off the map and was losing lives. Leo realised he had to push the others off the map to win the Fall Guys game. He pushed everyone off and won the challenge and returned home to his family.

Leo Forsyth (10)
Crawforddyke Primary School, Carluke

DAN AND THE POT

Once there was an explorer called Dan. While exploring an island one day, he saw a pot lying in the sand. Dan took the pot home.

When he got home, he desperately tried to open the pot. He failed. Dan tried for hours. It was now late and dark. Dan called it a night and went to bed. All of a sudden, a ghost popped out, looked at the house, and decided to do something unusual. When Dan woke up, it was super hot. He was in a new house in Australia. Confused, Dan saw the pot was gone!

Kayla Kinsella (9)
Crawforddyke Primary School, Carluke

THE LOST MERMAID

Anne wanted to go to the beach but her dad said no. When he wasn't looking, she snuck out to go to the beach. When she was sitting on the sand, a merman came out of the water and saw Anne. He swam up to her and said, "My name is Isaac and I think you are the lost mermaid."

Anne was in shock. She always wondered why her dad never let her go swimming! Anne went with Isaac to the lost city of Atlantis. She was astonished at who she met there. Her dad was also a merman!

Harry Cunningham (10)
Crawforddyke Primary School, Carluke

THE TEST

It started off as a normal day in World War II. Suddenly, a big alarm went off. Everyone panicked and screamed, people were struggling to put on gas masks because the gas was coming closer but then someone breathed the gas in. Nothing happened. Out of nowhere, bombs came flying in. But when they hit the ground, they turned into water. It turns out everything was a test. The gas, the bombs and the war were all a simulation that everyone was stuck in and couldn't get out of.

Mya Hunter (11)
Crawforddyke Primary School, Carluke

SNOW RED

One day in the dark forest, there was a girl called Snow Red. She was dancing with seven dwarves, then one of the dwarves pushed her. Snow Red pulled a knife out of her pocket and stabbed him. The other six ran, but Snow Red caught up and stabbed another one. Then she threw the knife away and pulled an AK-47 out of her hair. Then she shot two more. She shot one in the head and found a grenade and blew up the final two. Then the police turned up and shot her in the head.

Alan Steele (11)

Crawforddyke Primary School, Carluke

THE MONSTER FROM PARIS

Paris was known for its history with monsters, one was defeated last year. I was walking over to the Eiffel Tower. It was quiet, too quiet. I was sitting on the grass when a tall figure appeared at the top of the tower. It stared down at me with a terrifying look. I crawled over to my stuff in a panic and ran. It jumped off from the very top and chased me.
"No, leave me alone!"
It grabbed me with its long arms and that's how I disappeared, forever...

Daniela Hunter (11)
Crawforddyke Primary School, Carluke

ON MY WAY HOME

I was coming out of school like normal. I was with Amy. I would usually walk home with my auntie Kirsty, but this time, I didn't.

We were nearly home, just one street away. Then we turned the corner and saw a huge monster. It was so scary! Amy ran up to it but then the monster grabbed her. Eventually, the monster let her go. We ran and ran and ran away.

We finally got to my house, and after that, nothing. No one saw it ever again. No one knows where it is.

Millie Forrest (11)
Crawforddyke Primary School, Carluke

STRANDED ON THE ISLAND

Once upon a time, a boy called Jack was stranded on an island. He didn't know two bears were on the island with him. Jack fell asleep.
He was woken up by a growl. He opened his eyes and he was frightened. A bear was standing in front of him. He thought the bear was going to eat him... But the bear surprisingly gave him a hug. Then it got a fish from the sea and killed it. Then the bear gave it to Jack and Jack took the scales off and ate it.

Megan Dargie (11)
Crawforddyke Primary School, Carluke

THE ELF'S DILEMMA

Once upon a time, an elf called Phil was working in Santa's workshop. He was wrapping an enormous present when he ran out of paper. He went to the elf shop to buy some, but when he got there, his pockets were empty. He was very sad.
He walked past Santa's workshop and saw wrapping paper beside a gold sledge. It was a present for Mrs Claus. Santa was fast asleep. Phil was in a pickle. Should he steal the wrapping paper or wake Santa Claus?

Charlie Gray (10)
Crawforddyke Primary School, Carluke

JAMAL THE HERO

Two fishermen were on a boat in the ocean doing paperwork for their business when they dropped a shipmate called Jamal into the sea.

When he was sinking into the water, he popped a bubble which saw him gain musical powers. Unfortunately, it caused a tsunami.

Jamal made himself really big and blocked the water from reaching the beach where people were playing with their families. Jamal saved the day by pushing the water away!

Jay Young (11)
Crawforddyke Primary School, Carluke

AVA AND THE ALIENS

One day, there was a girl called Ava. She lived in a castle with her mum, dad and two sisters. Ava believed in aliens but her sisters always said aliens were not real.

But one morning when she woke up, she was in space in a castle with aliens. Ava thought it was fun until she realised she missed her family.

Then when she woke up the next morning, she was back in her own house, but her family were aliens.

Ava Brewer (10)

Crawforddyke Primary School, Carluke

BOY VS MONSTER

One day, a school went on a school trip.
When they arrived, they were at a theme park.
They were having so much fun. They all went on
rides. They all went on the biggest ride at the park.
It was 220 feet tall! Some of them bought food.
But then a really big monster came in and broke
all the rides. One kid called Kevin started fighting
and then he won against the monster and
everyone was so happy.

Lewis MacDonald (11)
Crawforddyke Primary School, Carluke

THE MYTHICAL BEAST

In a jungle surrounded by colourful ores, there lives a mythical beast. This beast has a spiky shell and a slimy body. It uses its snout to devour any living creature in one gulp. Anyone who dares hunt it down is never seen again. I have tried to capture it myself but have failed every time. However, I know a secret about the beast that nobody else knows. The secret is that I am the mythical beast.

Gregor McNeill (11)
Crawforddyke Primary School, Carluke

A TWIST YOU WOULDN'T EXPECT

It was a regular day for Star. Supervillains and superheroes were fighting for good or evil. Star always went on walks. She was just about to unlock her door when someone grabbed her and then everything went black. She woke up in a dark basement next to the hero, Angel. The villain came in and took their hood off. It was Star...
So who was the Star next to Angel?

Neve Clark (11)
Crawforddyke Primary School, Carluke

THE MYSTERY BOAT

I was on a boat. Suddenly, I noticed a giant rock ahead. "Watch out! Rock!" I shouted. The captain just blanked me. It was closer now. I hugged my mum tightly and shut one of my eyes. I thought we were about to die, but we didn't. I felt as if my insides were spinning as we went right through the rock into another dimension, never to be seen again...

Lacey Laird (11)
Crawforddyke Primary School, Carluke

JACK'S MAGICAL EXPERIENCE

Cautiously, Jack clambered up the long, twisty beanstalk. When he was getting near the top, he heard a thunderous, "Fee-fi-fo-fum!"

After he reached the top, he found a gigantic, brick castle with a weird-looking green flag flying from the tallest turret. Jack saw two enormous, wooden doors. He found a circular door knocker, which he pounded into the door.

The door creaked open extraordinarily loudly and there stood... The famous Harry Potter!

Recovering from his shock, Jack asked, "How did you make your voice so loud?"

Harry pulled out his wand.

"It's magic! Lengardiosa Fizz!"

"Wow! Impressive!"

Oliver Mackay (9)

Dorridge Primary School, Dorridge

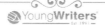

ALWAYS ASK A DOCTOR

Beauty had been asleep for a week, nobody knew what the problem was. The best fairies had visited, but they couldn't solve it.

One day, the head fairy suggested only true love's kiss could wake her. The king said, "We'll search the land for a prince!"

The Queen wasn't sure.

They finally found him. But when he saw the sleeping princess, he was unsure about kissing her. "We've never even spoken!"

The door opened. Dr Kirkbride confidently approached Beauty and gave her an injection.

"It isn't a man you need, darling, it's antibiotics."

Beauty woke and the doctor was promoted.

Indie Kirkbride (9)
Dorridge Primary School, Dorridge

MEAN MATILDA

Matilda hated books. She always had. Glued to a screen, she watched all day. Matilda had gone to school since she was 3, yet she was still in Year 1 (even though she was 8!).

She wailed the whole way to school. Every. Day.

"Matilda, quieten down!" said Mum, agony draining from her voice.

Late to school, she knew the drill. Go to Miss Trunchbull, get a slip, go to class.

"Hello, buttercup!" stated Miss Trunchbull.

Matilda didn't answer.

"Off you trot then," she encouraged.

Matilda slumped down to class where she was greeted by Miss Honey bellowing, "You're late!"

Darcy Churchill (10) & Aarya Mistry
Dorridge Primary School, Dorridge

THE TWO BEAUTIFUL DRAGONS

Once upon a time, there were two beautiful dragons who left home to live in their own caves. Each cave had a protective shield.

An evil spirit came by the first dragon's house.

It shrieked, "Let me in!"

The dragon replied, "Not by the sparkle of my horny-horn-horn!"

It shot and broke in. The dragon flew off to her sister's house but the evil spirit followed.

The spirit knocked and shouted, "Let me in!"

Both dragons replied, "Not by the glimmer of our horny-horn-horns!"

The spirit shot but couldn't break in, so they captured him and lived happily ever after.

Katy Quest (9)
Dorridge Primary School, Dorridge

THE BANDIT SNAKE-DRAGON

Once there lived a beautiful butterfly, her name was Sabrina. She lived in an ancient tree with special powers.

One stormy night, Sabrina was woken by a snake-dragon who stole the tree's heart. Without it, the tree would die, and the entire forest would also perish.

Sabrina found the dragon's underground lair. She knew she couldn't defeat the snake-dragon as a tiny butterfly, so she called upon all the butterflies in the forest.

At midnight, a million wings flew into the dragon's mouth, killing the beast! Sabrina took the heart back to her tree and saved the forest from destruction.

Izzy Mattine (7)
Dorridge Primary School, Dorridge

HARRY POTTER AND THE SORTING HAT DISASTER

It was Harry Potter's first day at Hogwarts and he was excited to get there. Yesterday, he went to London to buy everything he needed for school. He'd arrived at Hogwarts 20 minutes ago and was now ready for the Sorting Ceremony. The Sorting Hat called Harry's name. Harry took longer to be chosen. Eventually, the hat screamed, "Slytherin!" Inside Harry's body, he was shouting, "Nooo!"

All he could hear was wailing, shouting and screaming from the hall. He thought he would do the wrong things in Slytherin, but he just hoped things would be alright in the end.

Elinor Smith (8)

Dorridge Primary School, Dorridge

ARIEL'S NIGHTMARE!

We're all aware of the story of the Little Mermaid. She lives a good life under the ocean, blah, blah! In this story, she lives a long, horrible life in the dreadful Ursula's home, sweeping, dusting and weeping. She was supposed to live with Prince Eric but that didn't work out.

Meanwhile, Ursula was devising a way of telling her 'slave' that she was her mother...

Her 16th birthday was approaching and she would soon begin to turn purple, so she couldn't put it off anymore. She finally found the courage to blurt out the words, "Ariel, I'm your mother."

Avaani Sandhar (9)
Dorridge Primary School, Dorridge

THE THREE LITTLE PIGS AT CHRISTMAS

Christmas Eve was cold and frosty in the little pigs' brick house. Their other two houses had been blown down by the Big Bad Wolf. They hung three stockings above the fireplace, hoping for Santa, but didn't light the fire. They didn't want to hurt their special visitor and went excitedly to bed, hoping he'd come.

At midnight, when the pigs were sound asleep under their bedclothes, there was a thud on the roof. Suddenly, down the chimney appeared... The Big Bad Wolf! He whispered, licking his lips in anticipation, "I know what I want for Christmas: Pigs in blankets!"

Ben Frowd (9)

Dorridge Primary School, Dorridge

101 NEW COLLARS

There were once 101 Dalmatians captured by a devilishly cruel woman with black and white hair. She wanted to make a coat out of their fur but she had underestimated these cute little pups.

Three days after she had captured the spotty dogs, she mysteriously disappeared. Our clever canines returned home as if nothing had happened... except, they weren't wearing collars before, now they were all wearing black and white ones. The collars looked as though they were made from human hair. No one knows what happened to her really, but if I were you, I'd *never* trust a Dalmatian!

Rosa Baillie (9)
Dorridge Primary School, Dorridge

THE THREE EVIL GHOSTS

Once upon a time on a dark, spooky night that happened to be Halloween, there lived three creepy, scary ghosts. A blast of magic shot them out of a dark, black grave!
Terrified, the three ghosts could not get back inside, so they decided to scare the town instead! They crept quietly into the town, excited to frighten everyone and steal their yummy, delicious sweets. They were able to scare everyone, apart from a boy who just wouldn't scare.
He decided to scare them away instead! Horrified, the three ghosts ran away and the people lived happily ever after.

Ben Quest (7)

Dorridge Primary School, Dorridge

SANTA'S LIFE

It was Christmas Eve and Santa was getting his presents ready. 1,000,000 bags of coal, 100 presents! When he went into one nice child's house, Santa gave him coal. The kid awoke and saw coal! With the help of friends, he decided to build a team to save Christmas. They saw Santa had a big blue coat. Giant elves chased them. They eventually wrapped the elves in paper and hopped onto Santa's motorbike. Without warning, a boxing match began. In, out... Oooo! Santa punched but yay! The kids gave him a knuckle sandwich and he fell off! Christmas was saved.

Isaac Herd (9)
Dorridge Primary School, Dorridge

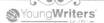

SCRUMPDIDDLYUMPTIOUS CHARLIE

Charlie Bucket opened the Scrumpdiddlyumptious bar Grandpa had bought for his birthday. He *really* wanted a golden ticket. He tore open the wrapper, there was no ticket. He started crying. His family were so poor and he was so hungry. He suddenly saw something glimmering in the snow - it was a coin! He thought about spending it on another Scrumpdiddlyumptious bar, but he saw a homeless man and gave it to him to buy a hot drink.
Two days later, the man came back to Charlie and said he'd won the Lottery and wanted to split it with Charlie.

George Ward (9)

Dorridge Primary School, Dorridge

THE FRIENDLY DRAGON

A dragon lived in a cave overlooking a village. She looked like a huge Komodo dragon with armour-plated scales, claws as long as swords, and teeth as sharp as razors. The villagers were scared of her. They offered a reward of £1,000 to whoever could slay the dragon.

A knight came who said he could get the dragon for them. He went to the cave. The dragon saw him and opened her mouth. The fire built up inside her mouth and the knight braced himself for his impending death...

Then the dragon said, "Would you like a cup of tea?"

Elanor Liddiard (8)
Dorridge Primary School, Dorridge

SLEEPING BEAUTY

The kingdom was full of joy, a princess had just been born and a party was being held to celebrate. Eleven fairies came and each one of them gave her a gift. All was well, until near midnight when a twelfth fairy came barging in, crouched beside the cradle, and whispered, "Bria-Rose, pretty and bright, on your birthday at night. You shall die, my oh my."
Sixteen years passed and a strange figure drifted into the room. They handed Bria-Rose some flowers and said bye. She felt something against her finger, hidden in the roses. She died.

Elizabeth Blight (9)
Dorridge Primary School, Dorridge

GEORGE'S MARVELLOUS MEDICINE

George's parents went out. He was left with evil Granny - she was being really mean! He decided to make a medicine in a big pan. George's mixture included shampoo, paint, polish, perfume and nail varnish. He put it in Granny's cup of tea.
Whilst George went to get a biscuit, Granny swapped the mugs around. Oh no! He drank the wrong drink and strange things happened. He started to get bigger and bigger... He was as tall as his house! Even though this hadn't been his plan, he was so big he could squash Granny like a fly! Yippee!

Charlie Ward (7)
Dorridge Primary School, Dorridge

JACK AND THE CARROT

In a village called Giant Stalk, lived Prince Jack. He wasn't a good prince. He would steal from the poor even though he was rich.

One day, a beggar woman asked for some money and Jack stole her bag. There were only seeds in it, so he threw them in the toilet.

The next day, a big carrot was poking out! He tried to pull it out, but got sucked down the toilet and got captured by dwarf rabbits. The beggar woman appeared and turned into a princess.

She said, "You will be my prisoner until you can be kind."

Persia Athena Vassell (7)
Dorridge Primary School, Dorridge

WISH, WISH, WISH

Annabel was walking home from school when her phone buzzed, startling her. She got out her phone and it was a reminder to say her birthday was today. Racing home, she went in and saw the most fabulous cake. Blowing out her candles, she wished for magical powers. As she went to bed, she waited for the magic.

The next day came without powers. She waited a week, but no! Just before Annabel was going to lose hope... *Powers!* She couldn't believe her eyes. She actually had magical powers and she knew it was that wish!

Amber Nyland (9)
Dorridge Primary School, Dorridge

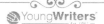

RUDOLPH THE GREEN-NOSED REINDEER

Rudolph the green-nosed reindeer had a very snotty nose and if you ever saw it, you would even say it was gross. All of the other reindeer used to fuss and give him tissues. They never let poorly Rudolph join in any reindeer chores.

Then one sunny Christmas Eve, Santa came to say, "Rudolph, blow your nose so tight. Will you go at the back tonight?"

Then all of the reindeer hated him and they cried out together in fear, "Rudolph, the green-nosed reindeer, you'll sneeze down the back of me!"

Emma Herd (7)
Dorridge Primary School, Dorridge

SNOW WHITE AND THE WICKED DWARFS

Snow White had a wicked stepmother who was jealous of her and wanted to kill her, so she ran away to the forest and was rescued by seven dwarfs. They told her that she must cook and clean if she wanted to stay.

One day, her stepmother disguised herself as an old lady and visited Snow White to give her a poisoned apple. Snow White knew it was a trick and saved it for later to make an apple crumble for the dwarfs. They ate the crumble greedily and dropped dead. Snow White lived happily ever after in their house.

Orla Jackson (8)

Dorridge Primary School, Dorridge

GEORGE'S DISASTROUS MEDICINE

Once upon a time in a grassland far away, a boy and his family lived with an evil grandma. His parents went out, leaving George alone with Grandma. She talked about the disgusting stuff she ate, amongst other weird things, so George sped into the kitchen! He decided to make a medicine! He could do loads of things. *Would she blow away with a gust of wind?* He put some bits inside a pot and gave it to Granny... she started to get more evil! She called him a mean boy. Then she ran away, never to be seen again!

Matty Pensom (7)

Dorridge Primary School, Dorridge

THE GIANT AND THE BEANSTALK

The giant lived in the castle with a magic chicken and a golden harp. He was scared of human beings, so he put the castle on a giant beanstalk he had found.

Jack crept up the beanstalk, went into the castle and tried to steal the chicken. The giant saw him and shook because he was scared.

He squeaked, "Fee-fi-fo-fum!"

This meant: 'Oh help me' in the giant's language.

The giant ran away but Jack cut down the beanstalk. The poor giant had a bump on his head and felt sad.

Samuel Hill (5)

Dorridge Primary School, Dorridge

THE LION THAT HAD NO VOICE

Once upon a time, there was a lion who was fun and playful. Sadly, he got bullied because the other lions were annoyed with him being a chatterbox. He just loved chatting. So he stopped to become their friend. How could the king of the jungle not roar? He knew he needed to guard his people. Every day, his friends tried to get him to roar but he just couldn't.

One day, without warning, he was playing flip the pancake with friends when it fell on him. He just smiled and... let out a massive roar!

Alexandria Hogan (9)

Dorridge Primary School, Dorridge

HARRY POTTER: THE SLYTHERIN

Once upon a time, there lived a boy called Harry Potter. He lived in a dull house and the family he lived with were the Dursleys.

One day, a giant named Rubeus Hagrid burst in and told Harry he had a place at Hogwarts School! When Harry got there, he was surprised because he didn't know about the Sorting Hat. Harry also didn't know that he was in Slytherin for his house. His best friend was Draco Malfoy and his enemy was Ron Weasley. Harry was very adventurous and was sometimes a bully!

Dylan Campbell (8)
Dorridge Primary School, Dorridge

THE THREE WEREWOLVES

Once upon a time on the outskirts of a small village, there lived three werewolves. Each built a house of their own. A house made of straw, a house made of wood and a house made of metal. A mischievous little piggy was out for a walk and stumbled upon the magnificently built houses. He decided to play a trick on the werewolves. He blew down the straw house, he punched down the wooden house and he tried to kick and knock down the metal house, but he hurt his fists and legs, so he ran home to his mummy.

Mason Bains (8)

Dorridge Primary School, Dorridge

THE THREE BEARS

One day, three hungry bears were on a walk through the forest when they came across a bungalow. Daddy Bear knocked on the door. No one answered, but the door creaked open, so they thought someone had opened it. So Daddy Bear went first. Mummy Bear followed. The little bear was scared, so took her hand.

All of a sudden, the door slammed shut. A little girl appeared in the distance. She attacked them and kept them in her basement, but what she didn't know was that the window was wide open. They escaped and never went out ever again...

Eliza-Mai Collings (11)
Edith Moorhouse Primary School, Carterton

THE WOLF

At Christmas, a big hungry wolf went around scaring people and trying to eat them. Then he got tired because he couldn't get anyone, so he ate an apple off the apple tree. When he ate it, he felt a bit weird. He looked down at himself and he was all green and hairy. He instantly knew who he had turned into... The Grinch! He was horrified. He ate a banana and turned back to his normal self. After that, he found the three little pigs' house. As soon as the little pigs saw the wolf, they charged at him...

Joseph Cutler (10)
Edith Moorhouse Primary School, Carterton

THE WITCH IN THE SKY

Once upon a time, a witch appeared in the sky. The witch kept forty wolves as pets. She started to howl and all the wolves came. They scared everyone back into their homes. The wolves went into their homes and killed everyone.

Soon, they began to explore and they found a room. In the room were forty swords. So the witch took all of them home. The wolves didn't kill any of the babies. They all lived as a nice family until the babies grew up and wanted to kill the witch for what she had done to their families.

Tiffany Hutton (9)
Edith Moorhouse Primary School, Carterton

BILLY GOATS GRUFF

One day, there were three goats. They had no grass in their field, so they wanted to cross the bridge to get to the other field so they had more grass to eat. However, they knew that there was a massive monster underneath and he was mean. They asked him if they could across to the other field but he said no.

So the goats made a plan to get past him. They knocked down three trees and put two of them over the bridge and one over the water. Just as they thought they'd crossed over, he climbed up...

Charlie Crutch (10)
Edith Moorhouse Primary School, Carterton

GOLDILOCKS

Goldilocks was walking through the forest. She saw a house. She decided to go inside. She saw three bowls of porridge, so decided to try them because she was hungry. One was too hot and the second was too cold. Then she heard a noise and saw claw marks on the wall. She was so scared, she decided to hide. She was also very tired, so she lay on the bed but it was too hard. The second bed was too soft, but then she heard the floor creak. The bears jumped out and trapped her in a cage.

Louie Paul (10)

Edith Moorhouse Primary School, Carterton

GOLDILOCKS AND THE THREE BEARS

Twice upon a time, Goldilocks went back to the three bears' house as her little brother had gone missing. She thought one of the bears had taken him. The last time she was at the house, there was not a basement. She went down the stairs and she saw... The three bears. But the next thing she saw was not what she wanted to see. It was her brother. He was on the ground after being hit. He woke up and the bears attacked him with their claws. She ran, leaving him behind...

Rosie Goodman (10)

Edith Moorhouse Primary School, Carterton

TOP GUN PORTAL

Maverick was fixing his plane when he got zoomed into a portal and soon appeared in a plane dreamland. There were F-18s and a Northrop. He was just chilling until a weird image appeared in front of him. It was another portal. He ran as fast as he could, but the portal sucked him in.
Before long, he was on the other side. He thought he was safe until a dinosaur started chasing him. It didn't chase him for long though. He found a jet and flew all the way home.

Charlie Sprigg (10)
Edith Moorhouse Primary School, Carterton

FLY AROUND THE UNIVERSE

5, 4, 3, 2, 1... Blast-off! The NASA ship had taken off. Astronaut Timmy was onboard. Only the top part had been deployed, but the back bit didn't go down. Instead, it started following us. We turned and swirled, and we did a loop-the-loop. We even went around Saturn. It was still following us, so we went around Jupiter, Mars, Earth and the moon. It was still following us. Then we went through a portal and crashed into the Atlantic...

Finley Agar (9)
Edith Moorhouse Primary School, Carterton

A TWIST IN THE DINOSAURS' TALE

The dinosaurs were about to be wiped out. A meteorite was going to kill them all. *Blam! Pow!* The meteor exploded mid-air! They were saved! But... there was a spaceship flying towards them. Aliens. They gave the dinosaurs armour and blasters, made them fight and rode them like horses.

100 million years later, the dinosaurs were used to kill all humankind and aliens ruled the dusty wasteland Earth had become.

Jacob Austin (10)
Edith Moorhouse Primary School, Carterton

THE THREE LITTLE PIGS: WITH A TWIST

One day, a wolf arrived in Pig Village. The wolf enjoyed blowing down houses, especially pigs' houses. The three pigs got prepared for their house to be blown down.

The next day, the wolf found an apple in the mysterious forest and overnight, he turned into a bear called Grizzly. Grizzly decided to blow down the pigs' straw house. So the three little pigs started to make a wooden house...

Lily Price (10)

Edith Moorhouse Primary School, Carterton

THE TWIST OF A HAUNTED HOUSE

They all started to chat with people while the waiters started serving food.

"I'm not hungry, let's just not eat," Ivy said.

So they didn't eat. Everyone started eating though. It became hushed because everyone was eating. Suddenly, someone fainted! And another! The guests started fainting!

After a minute, everybody had fainted!

"Oh no! I'm glad we didn't eat anything. Let's go, it's spooky," April said nervously.

Just then, Ashley ate a piece of food from a tray! She fainted!

"No!" Ivy chanted dramatically.

They all got hold of Ashley and headed to the door. "It's locked! Oh no!"

Holly Fairless Bush (10)
Homerswood Primary School, Kirklands

RAPUNZEL: A TWIST

Rapunzel went down this unerring tube, which took her to an unwelcoming haunted house. When Rapunzel took her first step, it immediately turned eerie. It was even making her chillingly cold. "Arghh!" Rapunzel screamed.

She fell; through a doorway that she'd never see again. Whilst Rapunzel was nowhere to be seen, Mother Gothel was making her way to the haunted house to see what was happening to Rapunzel. "Hahaha!" laughed Mother Gothel, laughing her head off. She'd finally caught Rapunzel.

Suddenly, Rapunzel found a way out. By the time Mother Gothel realised, she was running. Then she vanished...

Annie Bailey (10)
Homerswood Primary School, Kirklands

THE FORBIDDEN PORTAL

The girls looked up and saw a huge, horrifying house. Surrounding it was a gigantic, creaky gate. They knew something strange had definitely happened. Daisy's house had never looked like this! The brave girls opened the gates in fright. They held hands and took large steps towards the house. Behind them, the mysterious gates slammed shut, locking them in a horror movie. There was nothing but smoke around them until the girls tried to clear it. Then the house appeared. There were crows flying around the building. Sophia shyly said, "Maybe it'll be better inside." The girls nodded in agreement.

Neve Kent (10)
Homerswood Primary School, Kirklands

AFTERLIFE ANGELS

One day, there was a girl named Freya who had ginger hair. She lived in a forest with her mum, her dad and her brother, Leo. Freya went to school as normal and met her friend, Jemima.

At lunch, Freya got called into the office.

"Freya, come to the office! I just wanted to say something," said Miss Garoghan, sobbing.

"Well, what is it?" said Freya, confused.

"Well, your family were in a car accident," said Miss Garoghan balling her eyes out.

Now, the only thing Freya saw were angels.

What will happen next?

Ruby-Mae Reed (11)

Homerswood Primary School, Kirklands

THE PIGS' SACRIFICE

Next, the wolf tied them up. The wolf then dragged them back to the cave.

"Why are we here?" questioned the pigs.

"Well, I'm going to make you into soup!" exclaimed the wolf.

As the wolf was talking to the pigs, they were quickly cutting the ropes. Then all of a sudden, the pigs ran for the trap. Not long after, the wolf ran straight to his own trap, trying to get the pigs. Finally, the pigs got the wolf onto the sacrificial altar. After he was sacrificed, the pigs chanted a twisted song, summoning Satan...

Joshua Bouma (10)
Homerswood Primary School, Kirklands

A STRANGE HOUSE

When Luke got home, he turned his Xbox on and loaded Fortnite up. Luke accepted the game request immediately. When they were both ready, the two fought, but when Bill lost, he was left crying on the sofa. Then Luke tried to load up another game but the screen fizzled a grey colour and two graves on some grass appeared. Then a bony hand with a little bit of green flesh dug out of the ground. Then the door creaked open and a bony, fleshy, green hand appeared around the wall. Luke screamed. Then the creature came around the wall...

Luke Johnson (10)
Homerswood Primary School, Kirklands

THE SCHOOL OF YOUR WORST NIGHTMARES

Everyone rushed to their classrooms. Maisie accidentally bumped into a student and... the kid broke! Maisie dropped all of her books and bolted. She ran like never before. All of a sudden, she tripped. Maisie glanced blankly behind her and her heart dropped.

"Maisie, that is not good, you running away!" shouted the headmaster.

"Sorry, I really did not mean to," muttered Maisie as they slowly walked back.

For the whole night, Maisie did not go to sleep. The wind howled through her window.

Mia Dring (11)
Homerswood Primary School, Kirklands

HICKORY DICKORY DOCK

Hickory Dock was the king of Grandfather Clock Towers with his brother, Prince Dickory Dock. They were eating dinner when a letter thudded through the door. It said that Hickory was invited to a party that night.

Later on, they danced and danced all night. Suddenly, Hickory collapsed. The two brothers rushed to the hospital.

At the hospital, the prince was told that the king wouldn't make it. The doctor said it was blood poisoning. Then Hickory had a flashback...

Charlie Brewis (11)

Homerswood Primary School, Kirklands

A WOLF AMONG US

Smoky ash rained down from the sky. Rustling interrupted Harry's train of thought. There was nowhere to go, unkept bushes prevented him from running away. Growling, a black figure emerged from the woods. Fanged claws spiked out of its hairy paws.

"Hello, Olivia," Harry smirked ominously. "Really fooled them back there, eh?" The fur disappeared from Olivia's arms. Long, thick strands of fur grew all along Harry's legs...

Bethany Sperring (11)
Homerswood Primary School, Kirklands

THE THREE BEST FRIENDS WHO WENT MISSING

When they got out of the wardrobe, they got teleported to a place called The Backrooms. They were terrified and they all wanted to scream.

Then all of a sudden, they all got chased by a huge goblin. Luckily, they all escaped into a small room in the corner. Then Fred said he wanted to go, but Bob didn't, so he killed him with a knife.

After about 30 minutes, they went to find the exit...

Henry Robins (10)

Homerswood Primary School, Kirklands

MATILDA'S SCHOOL DAY

Matilda woke up and got ready for school. Matilda's mum made her breakfast. Her mum made her pancakes. When Matilda finished her breakfast, Matilda's friend, Bella, came to Matilda's house to walk to school.

At the end of the day, Matilda was walking home when a dog came out of nowhere and pushed Matilda into a river.

"Arghhh!" said Matilda.

When Matilda got out of the river, she couldn't remember where she was. Matilda's mum started to get worried. She went out to look for her.

"Matilda, where are you?" she shouted.

"I'm here, Mum!" said Matilda.

"There you are."

Rose Hand (9)

Mauricewood Primary School, Greenlaw Mains

THREE CATS WITH POWERS

Froot Loops, Harley and Fluffy were watching a movie. Fluffy said, "We should go outside."
They said, "Okay."
They went outside and went for a walk. Then they saw a dog barking at them.
They ran and said, "A dog is barking at us!"
River said, "Don't be scared, I am friendly."
The cats said, "How do we know for sure?"
River said, "I promise."
They became friends. Then they remembered they had powers. They said, "Buildings."
Then they went and ripped all the buildings down.
But before they ripped down the pool, they went and played in it.

Marisa Harris-Mckenzie (9)
Mauricewood Primary School, Greenlaw Mains

THE PIGEONS AND THE SEAGULLS

"Oh, this is so relaxing."

"I know, right."

"Arghh! Help! Coo, Coo!"

Unfortunately, Millie, Enola and Jane got swooped up by the seagull bubbler and screamed, "Arghh!" The seagull was evil and happy. All the other pigeons on the top floor of the ship were shocked. Worryingly, the seagull driving the bubbler got distracted and crashed... *Bang!* The seagull bubbler fell on the left side of the ship and all the weight pushed the ship over. It crashed into an iceberg. Sadly, 1,563 pigeons died. But on the right side of the ship, the pigeons were happily safe and sound...

Lena Crooks (9)

Mauricewood Primary School, Greenlaw Mains

DOLL-E

Once there was a robot called Doll-E who lived in a place called Haywood Land. A girl called Layla said, "Stop destroying our land."
Surprisingly, she decided to try and convince him.
Doll-E said, "I'm never nice."
"But truly, it's not hard."
Layla went to his house and talked to him.
"Why do you hate this world?" she asked.
Doll-E said, "When I was younger, my mum hated living."
Layla said, "Okay, just be kind, it's more fun."
The next day, he went to Haywood City and said, "Okay, I'm sorry."

Holly Lumber (9)

Mauricewood Primary School, Greenlaw Mains

GOOD TO BAD

Birch Terrace had always been a beautiful neighbourhood with kind people. Everyone helped each other out and looked after their neighbours. However, on Halloween night everything changed. A group of evil villains had escaped jail and were headed straight for Birch Terrace. The villagers were petrified! The evil villains put a curse on the neighbourhood to stop it from going back to normal when Halloween ended. The villagers would never see daylight again. Vampires and zombies roamed the streets, destroying everything in sight. The poor villagers of Birch Terrace didn't know what to do. They needed help...

Kamya-do Caine (9)
Mauricewood Primary School, Greenlaw Mains

THE LITTLE MERMAID'S REVENGE

One day on the coast of Malibu, under the water in Atlantis, a young mermaid sipped her tea whilst planning revenge on Atlantis.

"I shall make Atlantis fall."

Knock, knock! went the door.

"Lights out," said her father.

That night, she collected bombs to help Atlantis fall. Then she crept outside. Suddenly, the water felt like acid. She turned into an immense polluted monster.

The next day, Atlantis fell and all the swimming merpeople were eaten by the red mermaid. Then she realised she had eaten her father. And for the rest of her life, she ruled in grief.

Nicole Lister (9)

Mauricewood Primary School, Greenlaw Mains

THE THREE HAMSTERS AND THE BIG, FAT, MEAN GUINEA PIG

On a lovely Tuesday, the two children and two adults went to the pet shop to buy a guinea pig. So they bought the fattest and biggest one there. When they got home, the hamsters were dancing in their cage. Suddenly, the evil guinea pig started fighting the three little hamsters.

"I'm going to eat you little hamsters!" shrieked the big, evil guinea pig.

"Noooo! Don't hurt us!" they said.

"Maybe we should stop fighting!" exclaimed the little hamster.

The big, fat guinea pig agreed and they became best friends and lived happily ever after.

Lillian Mason (9)

Mauricewood Primary School, Greenlaw Mains

THE SCHOOL TRIP

Danny walked to school, excited about the trip. Halfway there, they drove into a strange place like a forest, then the bus driver revealed the news, they were lost!

The next thing he knew, everybody was screaming. But Danny wasn't screaming. Danny was thinking. He tried to memorise the place because he thought he recognised it and then he realised it was his grandpa's old house.

His father told him about the house, so Danny wasn't scared. Suddenly, he heard a noise coming from his grandpa's old house. Then he saw an old man standing in the abandoned house...

Kai Steel (8)

Mauricewood Primary School, Greenlaw Mains

HELL'S BELLS SCHOOL FOR WICKED BOYS

Once upon a time, there was a teacher called Mr Jenkins and he was sent to Hell's Bells School for Wicked Boys.

"No," he said. "Anywhere but there."

But it was too late. He was thrown into a van that said: 'Hell's Bells transport' on the side.

When they stopped for petrol, he didn't notice there were *ten* teachers behind him.

When he got there, he thought it was the end of the world. His class was the most devilish class in Scotland. Trembling with fear, he opened the door.

"Good morning," a boy said...

Oliver Lavery (9)

Mauricewood Primary School, Greenlaw Mains

THE BUTTERFLY

Butterflies live once and soon fall and die.
Although not this one, he's lived long enough to
last a century. He still lives, remembering the day.
A fragrance of the memory...
"Look, look!" a voice said.
He took me to a little, quiet room. It was fancy too!
The betrayal...
I thought for a second and stated he was nice.
Swiftly, *wham!* I managed to escape from a *crush!*
"Come back here!" he raged, never to be seen
again.
As I pass the house, a sense of evil comes towards
me...

Harrison Trang
Mauricewood Primary School, Greenlaw Mains

THE SCARED GIRL

Once there was a girl called Lily who was in her room. She went downstairs and shouted to her mum, "I'm just going for a walk in the woods, bye!" And off she went to the woods.

When she got to the entrance, she took one step forward. Then she started running. She found a creature, then the creature turned around.
"It's a witch!" she shouted.

The witch started laughing. Then suddenly, she turned Lily into a snail.

An hour after that, she found a wizard and he turned her back to a human. Then she walked home in horror.

Aimee Davidson (9)

Mauricewood Primary School, Greenlaw Mains

THE SECRET FORMULA

SpongeBob and Patrick were walking to the Krusty Krab, but when they arrived, there was no secret formula. SpongeBob couldn't remember the recipe, so they went on a hunt for it. They travelled very far but they finally found out who had it. It was Plankton! They headed to the Chum Bucket and there it was.

Surprisingly, he had a customer. It was obviously because of the secret formula. SpongeBob quickly pulled his spatula out and started to attack Plankton. Then Patrick ran in and stole the formula. SpongeBob escaped! The Krusty Krab was back in business.

Eli Lumsden

Mauricewood Primary School, Greenlaw Mains

JACK AND JAMES GO TO SPACE

It's the day I've been waiting for, we're going to space. Two hours later, we're in space. I can't believe it. Look at the Earth, it looks amazing. Let's go and explore. Look, a space rock. Let's go back to the spaceship. Arghhh, what is that on the spaceship? It's eating the spaceship. We need to stop it. How? We'll have to think of something. It's coming towards us... We are in its stomach. Look, a way out! No, that is its bottom. We have to get out somehow. Fine, here we go! We get out. Back to the spaceship.

Connor Ewen (9)

Mauricewood Primary School, Greenlaw Mains

THE MYSTERIOUS SLIDE

One sunny afternoon, two children were playing catch in their garden. Suddenly, one of the children threw the ball too far and it bounced over the old fence. They both ran out of the garden and down the creaky stairs to chase after the ball. When they reached the ball, there was a mysterious bright light coming from a bush in the woods. They followed the light and discovered a colourful slide. Quickly, they slid down the curvy slide. However, they didn't land in the woods. Instead, they landed in a green pool. They had no idea where they were!

Sophia Aird (8)

Mauricewood Primary School, Greenlaw Mains

THE FACTORY

One day, a young boy called Charlie won a golden ticket. It was gold and it was shiny. He went to the chocolate factory. They arrived at the factory and met Mr Willy Wonka. He was wearing a pink hat. The chocolate room was the best room.

Suddenly, Mr Wonka shouted, "The chocolate is on my sweet grass! Let's go to the chocolate river!" The chocolate Viking boat was melting and everyone was crying. The pink boat was split into one hundred parts. Everyone had to swim to the loud inventing room. The tunnel was dark...

Mikolaj Szczesniak (9)
Mauricewood Primary School, Greenlaw Mains

THE THREE BOYS

Three boys were on a car ride to the airport and the whole car nearly flipped.
"Thank God, he missed the car."
When they got there, they all ran to Jay's new helicopter. They were all so excited, they got on it. As they went, Mike screamed, ''A tree!"
Derek screamed. Everyone reached for a parachute as the helicopter went down. Suddenly, Jay fell out of the helicopter! Everyone jumped and silence grew all around. Mike woke up in the hospital. He screamed before black broke around him. He dreamt of the crash...

Mason Stafford (9)

Mauricewood Primary School, Greenlaw Mains

PIXELS

Tom found a mysterious video game in his basement that was called '???' Curiously, he put it into his old Nintendo console. He felt a strange feeling in his hands. Suddenly, his hands transformed into pixels and his whole body started disappearing. When Tom opened his eyes, he was in a world of pixels. A pixelated dog was licking him. He realised it wasn't a real dog. It was an alien made of pixels that could morph into dogs. Tom chopped its head off and suddenly felt stronger. He became one of the pixels and could never leave again.

Alex McCreadie (9)
Mauricewood Primary School, Greenlaw Mains

THE AMAZING AEROPLANE

"Okay, we are in the air now and we would like to advise you to sit down in your seat, and air sporters, please sit down as well, thank you."

Boom! Boom! Boom! Boom!

"We don't know what just happened, but we have been hit. So everyone, please grab a parachute. We are going down!"

"Help! Anyone, seriously! We need help!"

Down goes the plane.

"That's it, we need jetpacks to get out of here and I can't fly with you, co-pilot!"

There goes the co-pilot...

Joseph Kirk (9)

Mauricewood Primary School, Greenlaw Mains

A FUN SURPRISE

Grace and her brother went to the airport to go to Tenerife. When they got there, they bumped into their cousins. At the check-in desk their mums gave them a plane ticket to scratch off a surprise. Underneath, it said where they were really going. They were all going on a family holiday to Orlando, Florida. Grace was so excited to go on holiday with her family and to visit all the theme parks. They shared a villa which had its own pool.

They all had the best holiday making memories together. Grace said it was the best surprise ever!

Grace Gibb (8)

Mauricewood Primary School, Greenlaw Mains

DO NOT ENTER

Once upon a time, there was a rabbit and his mum. The rabbit was called Fred. Fred was a forgetful boy. He and his mum lived in a forest, so when it was night-time, it was quite dark.

One day, his mum came to him and said, "Go take these carrots to your poor uncle."

"Okay," said Fred.

"And do not go through the woods as a shortcut."

"Sure," said Fred.

And off he went but he forgot what his mum said and ran through the woods. There, he met a wolf and the wolf killed him.

Sophia Pang (9)

Mauricewood Primary School, Greenlaw Mains

TOMMY AND THE ZOMBIE WAR

Once there was a boy called Tommy. He was five when he got framed. He was now in prison. The siren for danger blared.

Tommy's friend Jake said, "That's not for an escaped convict, that's for war."

Then a zombie came and bit Jake.

He yelled, "Run!" and fell to the floor.

Tommy ran to the woods and found an axe. Then a zombie came. Tommy hit it in the head with the axe. Tommy went to the lunch hall in the zombie's skin. He ate and then the zombie skin fell off. Tommy got bitten...

Ruaridh Scott (9)

Mauricewood Primary School, Greenlaw Mains

ALIEN ADVENTURE

Meet Dave. He lives in a sort of small house in town. He's always wanted a dog and shoes.
One day, he went outside and saw something zooming towards him. He dived out of the way and saw smoke bursting out of it. It was a dog, but no ordinary dog. It was an alien dog.
The dog said, "Up in space, there's a big, evil UFO and it's going to destroy you."
Then the dog grabbed him and zoomed into space. They ran to the self-destruct button, pressed it and went back to Earth safely, except for the aliens.

Jack Thorne (9)
Mauricewood Primary School, Greenlaw Mains

THE PANDA AND THE BUTTERFLY

Once upon a time, there was a lonely panda called Ollie. No one wanted to be his friend. But one day, a butterfly called Sky landed on his head.

"Hey, get off my head," said Ollie.

"I am sorry," said Sky, "I didn't mean it, I just wanted to be your friend."

"My friend?" said Ollie in excitement.

They went to get some food in Pixie City, then they went to get some ice cream. When they were done, they went to look at the stars. Then they went home and got some sleep.

Emeli White (9)

Mauricewood Primary School, Greenlaw Mains

THE MYSTERY OF THE LITTLE GIRL

One day, a girl called Lexi woke up in a big, black room. "Help!" she shouted.

She looked around and she found a hole in the woods. She was as cold as ice. It was so cold, there was snow on the trees. As soon as she got out, she saw a man and asked for help.

He said, "Come and get in my van."

So she got in the van and went to a house.

"Do you want some food?" asked the man.

"Yes, please," said Lexi.

The man was very nice and showed her a lot of warmth.

Emily Stewart (9)
Mauricewood Primary School, Greenlaw Mains

WISH GONE WEIRD

One day, Jane was crying because she was ugly. A magic fairy godmother appeared and said, "You can look good for one night."

"Yes, please," said Jane.

Now because she looked like this, she went to the ball. But when she was dancing, she turned into an ogre. Everyone was so scared of her, they did what she said. Now, she ruled the world, but she had no friends. She begged the fairy godmother to turn her back to normal and she did.

Jane now loves herself and will never be unhappy again.

Eve Hogarth (9)
Mauricewood Primary School, Greenlaw Mains

THE THREE LITTLE PIGS

One day, three little pigs left home to build their own houses. The pigs went to get weeds, grass and concrete to build their houses.

After they'd built their homes, the big wolf came and kicked the grass one down. The pig went to the house made of weeds. The wolf came and tapped it. The pigs went to the other house. The wolf had a chainsaw and tried to knock it down. Next, he climbed onto the roof and went down the chimney. His bottom was set on fire. He said sorry to the pigs and they became friends.

Katie Fraser

Mauricewood Primary School, Greenlaw Mains

MUM'S SECRET LIFE

Danny and his dad lived in a big mansion. They were very rich and had all the latest cars to drive. One night, they heard a noise. It was one of their fanciest cars starting up. Outside the window, they saw the robber escaping in the car. They called the police. There was a big chase and Danny and his dad watched.

When the robbers got caught, they discovered it was Danny's mum. She said she wanted to live as a robber and have a lot of money! Danny and his dad moved to a caravan where they were happy.

Aiden Salt-Mayhew (9)

Mauricewood Primary School, Greenlaw Mains

THE GINGERBREAD MAN

One day, a lady was making a gingerbread man. She opened the oven and *boom!* The gingerbread man was out. The lady ran after him. The gingerbread man ran past the lake.

Then he found the river and did something really risky. He jumped all the way over the river! Then the lady jumped all the way over too.

He was blocked by a wall. The gingerbread man was scared, but then he jumped all the way over. The gingerbread man said, "See you later, lady!" But then he fell into the water. Oh no!

Walter Gray (9)

Mauricewood Primary School, Greenlaw Mains

THE NASTY WITCH

A nasty witch known as Violet had done everything she could to annoy all the teachers in Allison academy. She and her cat Tabby were always up to no good. I don't know why she did it. One morning Violet woke up and went down to get breakfast and had a smelly sock in her breakfast. Maybe the teachers wanted revenge and did it. "Eww, who did this? Ugh, I'll get you back." That afternoon Violet got called to the headteacher's office and found out that the headteacher was the one who did it.

Emmy Allison (9)
Mauricewood Primary School, Greenlaw Mains

SHOCK AT MIDNIGHT

When I was four months old, my mother died suddenly and my father was left to look after me all by himself. I had no siblings. All through my boyhood, from the age of four months onwards, it was just the two of us. We lived in a broken-down caravan because we couldn't afford a house. One stormy night while we were sleeping, Mum broke out of her grave as a growling zombie! She promised she was friendly and wouldn't hurt anyone. However, she failed to mention that she had in fact killed Mr Hazel...

Lily Chamberlain (9)

Mauricewood Primary School, Greenlaw Mains

THE TWO MYSTERIOUS TWINS

There were two little twins called Jill and Bill. They had broke parents. And when I say broke, I mean broke. Anyway, Jill and Bill's dad, Hill, got a job. It involved robbing the bank. He was so desperate, he said yes, but they did bad things to him.

"You know what, I quit!"

They did not let him quit, but the two twins bailed him out. Then the two twins got caught, so they were forced to rob the bank!

Somehow, the bad guys got caught, or did they? Find out in the next one, bye!

Charlie Newby (9)

Mauricewood Primary School, Greenlaw Mains

MRS WOLF'S PANCAKES

One day, Mrs Wolf wanted to make pancakes. She counted her money, but wolves aren't good at counting, so she got some help from Mrs Chicken. She banged on the door and asked Mrs Chicken for help, but Mrs Chicken was scared that she would get eaten. So she slammed the door and went to count by herself.

Next, she went to the shop, but wolves aren't good at carrying things, so she got some help from the pigs and they told her how to make pancakes. Half an hour later, 500 pancakes were made.

Ayla Hill

Mauricewood Primary School, Greenlaw Mains

THE THREE LITTLE RABBITS

The three little rabbits were hopping through the scary woods. They had made a burrow to protect themselves from the Big Bad Fox. However, the mean fox was desperate to catch the rabbits. He tried to get into the burrow but he was too big. Next, he tried to dig a bigger hole but it was taking too long. Finally, he set up a trap to catch the rabbits but he didn't know that they had already set their own trap. When the Big Bad Fox looked down the burrow something jumped up and snapped his nose. Ouch!

Tamsin Dobie
Mauricewood Primary School, Greenlaw Mains

THE THREE LITTLE WOLVES

Once upon a time, there were three little wolves. They were getting a little old so it was time to move out. They built their own houses out of plastic, cardboard and metal. In their houses, the wolves had large fluffy coats, which the Big Bad Pig wanted to destroy. He tried to get into each house but the little wolves were too smart! They had put a great magic spell on the houses to make them invisible. However, the great magic would only last 5 minutes! The little wolves were running out of time!

Ella Vakaloloma

Mauricewood Primary School, Greenlaw Mains

SNAKES

Once upon a time, there was a kid called Josh. Josh was a big fan of snakes. He loved purple snakes the most.

It was December, around Christmas Time. Josh asked for a stuffed snake or an LED snake. Josh wanted a real snake but he knew that it was too dangerous.

Now, it was January. Josh was 8. Josh went out with his friends to the woods. He and his friends found a portal in the woods. They didn't want to go through it, so they decided to go through it tomorrow...

Callan McLean (9)

Mauricewood Primary School, Greenlaw Mains

THE LITTLE PIGS

There were two pigs. They got kicked out of their mum's house. They made two houses. One made out of straw and the other made out of logs.
One day, a wolf came. He was hungry and wanted bacon. The first house he went to was made out of straw. He huffed and puffed and blew the house down, along with the other wooden house. Then the pigs ran to their mum's brick house. The wolf couldn't blow it down. Stupidly, the pigs ran out the back and the wolf ate the pigs.

Riley Morrison

Mauricewood Primary School, Greenlaw Mains

THE BIG BANG

Once upon a time, there was a red fire dragon called Bob who had a green dragon brother called Bobby. They didn't know how to blow fire; Bob and Bobby had to practise.

The next day, the boys went outside to practise blowing fire. There was a car that had a million explosives inside, but they actually didn't notice it. They practised and they finally got it, but they blew their fire on the car and then... 3, 2, 1. *Boom!* Their dad saw it all...

Max Hill (8)

Mauricewood Primary School, Greenlaw Mains

A BOY AND A SHARK

Alfie lived with his mum by the beach.

One day, his mum booked a boat tour. Alfie and his mum went on the boat. They were having a good time on the boat. Then a shark attacked the boat. The shark was grey with a white fin on its back, but the shark had a friendly smile.

Alfie's mum screamed, ''Help!''

But the shark didn't attack Alfie.

In the end, Alfie and the shark become friends and they rode into the sunset.

Emily Robinson (9)

Mauricewood Primary School, Greenlaw Mains

SAM AND THE PORTAL

Once upon a time, Sam and Riley were climbing trees in the woods. They were playing hide-and-seek. "Found you!" said Sam.

Then a portal appeared and out of the portal came a person. "Help! He's got superpowers!" said Riley. Sam threw a stick at the person and the person went back through the portal.

Two minutes later, suddenly, the person fell out of the sky and destroyed the world. Then they all got lost in space.

Benjamin Taylor (9)

Mauricewood Primary School, Greenlaw Mains

ALIEN INVASION

Once upon a time, Bob and Jonathan were shopping when there was an alien invasion warning. Bob said, "Oh my god!"
Suddenly, a UFO abducted them and Bob woke up in space. With a super scared voice, Bob said, "Why are we in space?"
Suddenly, a spaceship came and got out a rocket launcher. Both Bob and Jonathan ran all the way to Mars. Surprisingly, they found a spaceship and shot all the aliens.

Connor Savage (9)

Mauricewood Primary School, Greenlaw Mains

THE THREE LITTLE BUNNIES

There were three little bunnies and their mum kicked them out of the house. The three little bunnies set off to find a field to build their houses. One built their house out of sticks. The other used cement. The other built theirs out of straw.
There was a wolf and he knocked on their doors to invite them to his pool party.
The little bunnies said, "Yes."
The bunnies and their friend had fun.

Ava Hunter (9)
Mauricewood Primary School, Greenlaw Mains

DANNY THE CHAMPION OF THE WORLD

When I was one year old, my dad died and my mum had to look after me. From then on, it was just the two of us. Me and my mum lived in an old crusty caravan. When I was a baby, my dad always washed me and fed me when my mum was away. Suddenly, Mum fell to the floor. Quickly, I grabbed my phone and called 911. The ambulance rushed my mum to the hospital to do some tests. I was in tears when I found out that she had died...

Arya Stark (8)

Mauricewood Primary School, Greenlaw Mains

THE TWO LITTLE FOXES

Once upon a time, there lived two little foxes who wanted to make their own houses with rocks and metal. One day, a big bad boar came along to the first little fox's house. He huffed and blew it down. Then he went to the last fox's house. He couldn't blow the house down, so he went down the chimney. The little fox said, "But the fire is on!" Down came the big bad boar and burnt his bottom.

Keira Birrell (9)
Mauricewood Primary School, Greenlaw Mains

THE BOAT

It was night-time. Danny was still awake. Danny went to go look at the sea, then his dad woke up. He saw Danny and then he shouted, "Danny, what are you doing?"
Danny said, "I can't sleep."
They had forgotten that the monster was sleeping. Suddenly, the monster got up. He was mad. He pushed the boat and then Danny and his dad fell into the sea. Then... they got eaten!

Lauren Macdonald (9)
Mauricewood Primary School, Greenlaw Mains

THE HOUSE WITH HISTORY

One day, there were three kids called Rath, Rose and Rachel. Their mum and dad were called Natalya and David. They saw this house and they loved it. They shovelled out all their money, just to buy it.

At first, they were so happy in the house, but one day at breakfast, David went to get the post. There was only one letter from an odd person. It did not say who it was from.

It is still unknown...

Freya Stephen (9)

Mauricewood Primary School, Greenlaw Mains

CAT IN THE HAT

One day, Cat in the Hat went out for a walk with Thing One and Thing Two. Cat in the Hat said that they needed some food, so they went to the shop and bought some food. Then Thing One and Thing Two wanted to go to the big sweet shop and get ice cream. Cat in the Hat said that they could go in and get some sweets, so they got some. Then they got tired, so Cat in the Hat took Thing One and Thing Two home.

Lauren Hill
Mauricewood Primary School, Greenlaw Mains

CINDERELLA

One day, Cinderella was a famous princess who lived in a hotel. Cinderella went down to the kitchen to get some food. Next, she went to the ball and she saw Prince Charming's wife. It was her evil sister! She didn't know. No one told her. She got mad at him and then she started running at him. They hated every day now...

Ellie Pearson (9)

Mauricewood Primary School, Greenlaw Mains

Young Writers Information

We hope you have enjoyed reading this book – and that you will continue to in the coming years.

If you're the parent or family member of an enthusiastic poet or story writer, do visit our website **www.youngwriters.co.uk/subscribe** and sign up to receive news, competitions, writing challenges and tips, activities and much, much more! There's lots to keep budding writers motivated!

If you would like to order further copies of this book, or any of our other titles, then please give us a call or order via your online account.

Young Writers
Remus House
Coltsfoot Drive
Peterborough
PE2 9BF
(01733) 890066
info@youngwriters.co.uk

Join in the conversation!
Tips, news, giveaways and much more!

**YoungWritersUK** 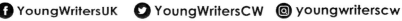**YoungWritersCW** 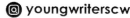**youngwriterscw**

 Scan me to watch the A Twist In The Tale video!